Maitland Public Library
501 S. Maitland Ave
Maitland, Fl 32751
(407) 647-7700

FULL SERVICE

WILL WEAVER

FARRAR, STRAUS AND GIROUX
NEW YORK

www.fsgkidsbooks.com

Library of Congress Cataloging-in-Publication Data
Weaver, Will.
    Full service / Will Weaver.— 1st ed.
        p.   cm.
    Summary: In the summer of 1965, teenager Paul Sutton, a northern
Minnesota farm boy, takes a job at a gas station in town, where
his strict religious upbringing is challenged by new people and
experiences.
    ISBN-13: 978-0-374-32485-8
    ISBN-10: 0-374-32485-9
    [1. Coming of age—Fiction.   2. Service stations—Fiction.
3. Farm life—Minnesota—Fiction.   4. Minnesota—History—20th
century—Fiction.]   I. Title.

PZ7.W3623 Fu 2005
[Fic]—dc21

2004057671

To my mother, Arlys Weaver,
with love

FULL SERVICE

I

One bright spring morning in 1965, my mother said suddenly, "Paul—what would you think of working in town this summer?"

"Me?" I said stupidly. She was washing breakfast dishes, I was drying, and we were listening to her little transistor radio—something about freedom riders in Alabama and teach-ins in Washington. At least I thought we were both listening.

"Yes, you. A summer job off the farm." Her gaze went to the kitchen window, and beyond it to our red barn, the shiny metal grain bins, the pale green fields stretching flat and far.

"You mean like last summer? Mowing those old ladies' lawns?" I hated being dropped off in town with my lawn mower. I felt stupid, naked, exposed—an interloper subject to attack by rough boys at any moment. That and the towering elms that cut off the sun, the houses a short clothesline apart, the little old ladies who peeked through their windows watching my every move—all of it depressed me. Especially the trash. The closer my mower came to the street, the more I had to watch out for it: cigarette butts, some with red lipstick stains; a broken and snarled eight-track tape; a smashed coffee cup; flintless cigarette lighters; once, a limp and floppy condom. When my mother came to fetch me, I was always exhausted and happy to go home to the farm.

"No, no, no," she said impatiently, wiping her hands and turning down her radio, "a real summer job—full-time. One where you could meet the public."

I glanced quickly through the screen door. "What about Father?"

"I'll talk with him."

I shrugged. "Yeah, well, what about the others?"

"For once let's not worry about *the others*," she said. She turned back to her dishes, and her hands again moved in the soapy water as quick as trout among stones.

"The others" takes some explaining. We were a Midwestern family long on religion. Not Lutheran, but sort of. Not Mennonite, but kind of. Not Amish, but a little bit. Not Quaker, but a good part. It was a Christian nondenominational faith, a phrase mystifying to my few school friends who were not in it ("Come on, Sutton, how can a church have no name?"). Farmwork was communal. My family shared the larger machinery—baler, grain combine, corn picker, silo-filling equipment—with several other families in the Faith. Planting, haying, threshing, silo filling, corn picking were done on an orderly circuit: VandenEides, Grundlags, Sorheims, Suttons (that was us), and so on. Unlike the Mennonites in Canada, or the Amish in central Minnesota, each family owned its own farm, but the focus was on shared work, worship, and fitting in with the others.

My mother hastily wiped her hands to turn up the volume on her radio. The tinny, scratchy voice of the newscaster could hardly be heard over people chanting and sirens wailing—a civil rights demonstration. "The world is changing, Paul, right this instant!"

I muttered something that she didn't hear. It was her most annoying habit—making sweeping statements about the world—because really she was talking about me. How I needed to be more "outgoing," more "social." I had a sinking feeling that "meet the public" was this summer's grand plan for me.

The morning stretched out endlessly, and as noon approached, I looked with increasing frequency at the clock. But that was not necessary. My father, Glen Allen Sutton, crossed the yard from the barn at exactly twelve o'clock. He was a medium-sized man with nut-brown forearms, oat-colored hair, and a ruddy face; he wore a clean work shirt every day, and long johns 365 days a year (woolen in the winter, light cotton in the summer). We waited while he washed up in the summer sink. His manner was deliberate—he always used all the same motions washing his hands, then rattling the roller towel.

At the table we bowed our heads as he gave his blessing: the beauty of spring, the parable of seeds falling on bountiful soil, our faith in their growth—and always the gift of good work. I peeked at my mother; she was peeking at me.

When grace finally ended she passed him the hot dish, then said in an offhand way, as if it had just come into her head, "Paul is thinking of working in town this summer."

I looked at her with instant annoyance.

My father turned to me. "Mowing lawns? Like last summer?" He carefully spooned scalloped potatoes and ham onto his plate; he could be starving and still not hurry.

"No. Something full-time," she said.

"Full-time?" My father's serving spoon stopped in mid-stroke like a mower's sickle against stone. His eyes opened to their full slate gray.

I cleared my throat. "Well, Father," I said, "I dunno, maybe not *full* full-time."

"You're needed here in the vineyards, son," he said. Leave it to him to find a biblical allusion.

"Yes, but I've been thinking," my mother said. "I have a plan."

"A plan," my father said, raising one pale bushy eyebrow at me. I looked away; I didn't want to take sides. However, my mother had a history of "plans"—the chinchillas, for example. "All that unused space in the attic," she had said enthusiastically, "think of the extra money we could make!" They were gone now, the furry little critters; their skittering and rattling and scratching about in their cages all night had driven us crazy.

"Yes, a plan," my mother said testily (we knew enough not to bring up the matter of the chinchillas).

"All right. I'm listening," my father said, though he really wasn't.

"First, Paul finds a job—a real job, one where he can meet the public—and then we hire someone to take up the slack here at home," she said.

My father reached for the bread. He began to butter a piece. The silence went on. Finally he said, "First, I don't know that Paul necessarily wants to work in town. Second, who could we find to take his place? There are no hired men anymore. But third, none of it really matters, because there aren't any jobs in Hawk Bend for farm kids. Town kids have them all."

There was silence. I looked down at my food.

"It must be nice to be right all the time," my mother said.

I sucked in a breath and held it.

My father put down his fork; he stared at my mother, then at me, as if we had conspired against him. Me, I was suddenly angry at both my parents; I had started none of this. "Go ahead and look around town," he said. "You'll see." Then he continued eating with the same even chewing motion. He had already moved on to something else inside his head.

The next day, I drove. Still over three weeks from my sixteenth birthday, I had a driving permit but not my license yet, which meant I needed an adult in the car. My mother, of course, was excited about our adventure. She insisted that I dress up, so here I was in a short-sleeved white shirt, clip-on tie, and school pants. At the stop sign for the highway, I waited for several tourist cars to pass, two of them pulling boats, and after them, a stubby, boxy motor home—rare enough to draw a second look. I waited for another car pulling a boat.

My mother fidgeted. "You could have made it, Paul."

"What's the hurry?" I muttered.

Soon enough we neared town. Even the faded city limits sign, with its rusty bullet holes, drew my eyes today. Hawk Bend, Minnesota (population 1,750), was a four-hour drive northwest from Minneapolis. It sat at the eastern edge of the Great Plains where a long-ago glacier had grated and scraped along, pushing all the rich black dirt into Iowa. In its path the glacier left behind lakes, chains of them, each surrounded by sandy shores and tall pines, lakes that were favorites of tourists from Minneapolis and St. Paul, from Iowa, the Dakotas, Illinois, and beyond.

Tourists came for the water, not shopping, so Hawk Bend remained small. It was ruled by a single traffic light at the central intersection. That and two older policemen who occasionally drove the perimeter, then circled back to Main Street, where they parked at either end and sat slumped in their sedans. Judging from their posture and their sunglasses, it was unclear whether they were awake. Despite a summer surge of traffic, Hawk Bend remained a small town with lots of churches, little crime, and clear if unwritten rules of summer employment.

Town kids worked in grocery stores or clothing stores. Farm kids worked at the very few jobs that remained: tossing bags at the feed mill, mixing dirt at the greenhouse, or pumping gas. There was a businessman's logic to this: town kids had the "gift of gab," but knew nothing of physical work; farm kids were too shy to sell anybody anything, but were used to hard work and were at ease around tools and machines.

I knew these rules in my bones, as did my mother, but nonetheless she first wanted me to look for a job "uptown." She waited in the pickup as I trudged into Kendrigan's Clothiers on Main Street. Barely inside the store I felt the silence and smell of fresh wool and shoe leather descend on me; I blinked as my eyes adjusted to the muted light.

"May I help you?" said Mr. Kendrigan himself; he leaned out from behind a male mannequin. A dapper middle-aged man, William Kendrigan was dressed à la mode in a powder-blue suit with narrow lapels and a red carnation; he had wavy bright-blond hair that was most certainly dyed. His eyes fell to my clip-on tie.

I looked about the store, which was silent, museum-like; I felt my throat closing. "I'm looking for . . . ties," I stammered.

"I should think so," he said. He guided me briskly, hand on my shoulder, toward a wire rack of wide bright ties. "Just give a shout," he said, then returned to work on his mannequin. His touch tingled on my shoulder.

Falsely I inspected the ties for what I thought was a reasonable amount of time, then slipped out the door.

"Any luck?" my mother said.

"No."

More likely a prospect was Bob's Mart, a brand-new warehouse-sized grocery store at the edge of town dressed with colored banners that crackled and snapped in the breeze. Unlike the gloomy cheese-smelling general store on Main Street, Bob's had no worn and undulating oak-strip floors, no ice chests, no butcher's shop at the rear where older farmers still delivered dressed hogs and sides of beef—none of that. Bob's was a modern supermarket where the food came frozen and from far away in semitrailers.

"I'll wait here," my mother said.

For which I was grateful. Who needs his mother along when applying for jobs? Especially if she's wearing a long dress and clunky old-fashioned shoes. In our religion women dressed simply. They wore no makeup or earrings, their hair was uncut and pinned up, their dresses simple and long. Men were clean-shaven and dressed unobtrusively. Unlike the Amish, whom we considered vain with their beards and severe black hats, we were true plain style. I could spot us a mile away, however, and figured that so could everyone else.

Inside Bob's Mart I squinted at the bright lights, listened to the rattle of cash registers. Each till was operated by a pert woman who looked fresh from a television show. The carry-out boys wore bow ties; all were town kids. I recognized several of them from school. Two smirked at me, whispered to each other.

I edged my way to the service counter and managed, with only a slight stammer, to ask for an application. I filled it out in full public view, then waited for the assistant manager, who I was told was in the freezer room.

He finally appeared wearing heavy gloves, a jacket, and a white, short-billed plastic hard hat; cool fog rolled off his back and shoulders. He glanced down at my application, then asked me a question or two. The unceasing movement, noise, and color of the store left me distracted and staring. "Later in the summer, maybe," I heard him say. I nodded dumbly and left.

Afterward, my mother suggested we take a break and stop at the Dairy Queen. There we licked our cones.

"Well, Paul, where to next?" she said at length.

I narrowed my eyes, scanning her face for even the faintest trace of sarcasm. There was none. I thought momentarily of her life; of her growing up in a religious farm family, then marrying my father, another farmer; I thought of the transistor radio she always listened to when he was in the fields. "We could try the feed mill," she said, "but there you might as well be back on the farm."

I was silent.

"How about the gas stations?" she said.

"Okay," I said without enthusiasm.

"The Shell station first," she added.

The broad yellow Shell Oil station sat at the main intersection of Hawk Bend—and its only stoplight. The

Shell station had the highest gas prices in Hawk Bend, and was known as the tourist's service station.

We both went inside.

"Sutton?" the owner, Mr. Davies, said, "as in the dairy Suttons from east of town?" He was a large-bellied man with small, soft, damp hands.

"Yes, sir," I said.

"We don't get many of you . . . folks looking for work in town," he added.

You folks: Bible thumpers?

Mr. Davies suddenly leaned closer. "How many teats on a dairy cow?"

"Four," I said, though it was occasionally five, even if the extra one was shriveled and dry.

He laughed largely, a Santa Claus laugh, and winked at my mother whose half smile remained unchanged. It was two o'clock in the afternoon and I could smell something sweet and strong on his breath. Whiskey, I was pretty sure. "Just checking to make sure you're a real Sutton. And your timing couldn't be better. I lost my regular day boy just last week, so the job is yours." He put out a damp hand once again. "A dollar fifty an hour, and you can start tomorrow."

"I can?" I said like an idiot. I suddenly tried to free my hand from his.

Behind me, my mother sucked in a small breath.

"One thing," she said. "Paul wouldn't be able to work Sundays."

"No problem," Mr. Davies said. "I've got a night

boy, Tim, and Kirk helps out on weekends. Be here to-morrow, eight a.m. sharp."

Of course you'll have to keep up with your chores at home, too," my father said at supper. A vein pulsed in his forehead.

I nodded. "I can keep up."

"I'll help him," my mother said. My father ignored her.

"And the haying, too," he added.

"The haying," I replied.

"And your Bible studies." He leaned closer and locked his eyes onto mine.

I looked down. I was studying toward "confirmation" (as the Lutherans called it) with two of our preachers, and things were not going well.

"Yes, sir," I mumbled.

"I'll help Paul as best I can," my mother repeated.

"You have everything else," my father said to her, gesturing sharply to the house, the garden, the flock of chickens that drifted beyond the barn. "I don't see how—"

"The Lord will provide," my mother said to him. "It's what you always say, yes?"

2

I began work Wednesday morning, eight a.m., on an empty stomach. I was too nervous for breakfast. My mother dropped me off at the station, handed me my lunch bag, and then drove away, making a point of not looking back. I turned to confront my new life.

The Shell station sat observed by three churches—Methodist, Lutheran, and Baptist—at the northeast corner of the intersection. It was a low yellow building faced with shiny tin panels. Above the front door was a yard-wide orange-and-yellow scallop, like a single eye with upraised brow, that stared back at the churches. Plate-glass windows looked out upon three pairs of squat, square gas pumps and two dusty black pneumatic bell cords that snaked across the driveway.

"Sutton!" boomed Mr. Davies from the doorway. "Let's go!"

I hurried inside.

"This is the manager, Kirk Johanason."

I shook hands with Kirk, a short, muscular fellow with a pale crew cut.

"Welcome to the salt mines, kid," Kirk said.

I nodded and managed a half smile. I knew of Kirk. He was a champion wrestler several years ago at the high school; he had gone to the state tournament in the 152-pound class, and now was married with two small kids. He drove a baby-blue two-door 1963 Chevy 327, one of the nicer cars in town.

"Wait here while I get your uniform," Mr. Davies said.

"Yes, sir." While I waited, Kirk ignored me, so I looked around. The long glass countertop was scratched by coins and tools; its shelves below were filled with souvenirs of Hawk Bend: tiny birch-bark canoes, rubber tomahawks, Paul Bunyan and Babe the Blue Ox salt and pepper shakers, agate key rings, aerial-view postcards, miniature metal license plates with twenty common names ("Al" through "Walt"), and bumper stickers ("There's no job like no job!"). Behind the counter was the till. An oil-smudged plastic sheet covered its keys. Beside the till was a bright stand-up display of Shell No-Pest Strips, insecticide bars sealed in foil wrappers like candy bars that made my nose itch. I stepped away from them. To the left, farther back, were wire racks of engine oil, purple cans of transmission fluid, half-pints of brake fluid, and a shelf of black twelve-volt auto batteries. At floor level were new tires, Goodyear whitewalls, their high, fresh-smelling treads bearded with tiny rubber whiskers. On the walls above were fan belts drawn together at their centers with short, numbered cardboard sleeves. The belts lined the walls like a hatch of giant dragonflies.

Mr. Davies returned from his little office. "Products

for every need," he said, spotting me scanning the office, "a need for every product. We pride ourselves on sales and service here, Sutton—Shell service. Let's get you into uniform."

"Yes, sir," I said, accepting a bag of clothing.

"Go in the can and put these on, Sutton. They belonged to Brian Tesker. He got drafted."

"Yes, sir," I said. Closing and locking the door behind me, I shed my clean (and pressed) jeans and shirt in favor of a rumpled Shell uniform: dark brown, wide-legged, wrinkled pants, a short-sleeved tan shirt that read "Brian" over the left pocket, and a bow tie with a couple of oil spots. The shirt was three sizes too large and smelled strongly of its previous owner.

"Don't worry about the name badge. You'll get your own soon enough."

"Yes, sir," I called, smoothing the wrinkles as best I could. In the dim, cracked mirror I straightened the bow tie, then stared at myself in uniform. My head had been transplanted onto another person's body.

"Do they fit, Sutton?" Mr. Davies' voice boomed close to the door.

"Sort of, sir."

"Well, if they don't, your mother can alter them," he said impatiently.

"Yes, sir." I kept staring at myself in the mirror.

"Let's take a gander, Sutton," Mr. Davies said.

I opened the door and stepped out.

Mr. Davies nodded. "Excellent. You're in the army now, son," he said. "Basic training starts with the seven-point Shell service code."

"Yes, sir."

"A road-weary driver sees the Shell sign from afar and what does that driver think?"

"Products for every need?"

"Shell gas. Shell oil. Shell service, that's what he thinks."

"Yes, sir."

"You come from a religious family, Sutton, right?"

"Yes, sir."

"When that driver turns in and pulls up to the pumps, it is an act of faith, Sutton."

"Yes, sir." Weirdly, I felt a small thrill run through me; my uniform, the Shell logos on my shirt, had strange powers.

"Faith in what, Sutton?"

"Shell gas, Shell oil, Shell service, sir."

"What kind of service?"

"The seven-point service, sir."

"Good, Sutton," Mr. Davies said. "Now repeat after me: Cheerful greeting."

"Cheerful greeting."

"Fill with ethyl?"

"Fill with ethyl?"

"Check oil."

"Check oil."

"Check water."

"Check water."

"Check radiator and fan belt."

"Check radiator and fan belt."

"Wash windshield."

"Wash windshield."

"Provide extra service."

"Provide extra service."

"You're going to go far, Sutton."

"Thank you, sir."

"But what about number seven, Sutton, extra service?"

I waited.

"What do you think that means, Sutton?"

"Extra service?" I ventured.

"Precisely," Mr. Davies boomed. "You notice something—dusty headlights, an overflowing ashtray—and you take the initiative, Sutton."

"Yes, sir."

"A loose hubcap, you pound it back on."

"Yes, sir."

"Extra service is what separates the men from the boys in the great Shell family, Sutton."

"Yes, sir."

Mr. Davies leaned forward, lowering his voice. "It is also what could win you one thousand dollars."

My eyes widened.

"Shell, Incorporated, never sleeps, Sutton. There

are Shell stations across the world. This may be Hawk Bend, Minnesota, but my station is no different from a Shell station in Parlez-Vous, France; in Sprechen Sie, Deutsch; in Coon's Butt, Kentucky."

I nodded.

"And how," Mr. Davies said, leaning forward still closer (his coffee-and-whiskey breath made me squint my eyes), "do you think Mr. Shell keeps track of all his stations?"

"I don't know, sir."

"He visits them, Sutton."

"He does?"

"Indeed he does, Sutton. Mr. Shell visits every one of his stations. You won't know when. You won't know his car. You won't know what he looks like, but one day Mr. Shell will come."

Goose bumps swirled across my forearms.

"However, you will not know he is Mr. Shell until afterward," Mr. Davies said, leaning closer to me. "Only afterward will he reveal his identity. But if you have performed the seven-point service plan—to his satisfaction—you will win, Sutton, one thousand dollars!"

At that very moment the driveway bells dinged; a car pulled up to the pumps. I froze, then looked at Mr. Davies.

"You're a Shell man now, Sutton!" Mr. Davies thundered. "Go get 'em!"

I sprang through the doorway.

Not much later, after Mr. Davies left the station, Kirk said, "Don't get sucked into that 'Mr. Shell' bullshit."

I stared.

"I've been here three years and no friggin' Mr. Shell has ever come."

I was silent, then said, "But he could come."

"Mr. Shell?" Kirk stared at me, then began to laugh. "Don't you get it? There probably ain't any Mr. Shell." He laughed so hard he began to cough. Taking a key from the till, he went to the pop cooler and opened the lock. He rattled a bottle of RC Cola along the slots, popped off the cap, and slugged half of it down.

Kirk noticed me staring.

"Want one?" he said.

"No, thanks."

"On the house. The old man's gone, help yourself."

I shook my head.

Kirk sighed. "You're one of *them*. All right, come on, I'll show you the back room."

If the front office was well lighted and generally clean, the back room was a dark noisy dungeon. The tool bench was constructed of heavy pine beams long soaked through from oil, and battered from hammers and wrenches. Centered in the back room was the hydraulic hoist: a single shining column, as thick and smooth as a peeled pine tree, that rose from the floor. Powered by a thudding air compressor and hydraulic fluid, the iron arms of the hoist held up a Buick without complaint. To the right of the hoist was the tire machine; it looked like a torture seat, a backless chair with an upright spike and a pneumatic arm. Beside it, hung on the wall, was an array of curved picks, levers, pincers for removing foreign bodies from tire treads. A box of offenders lay there: nails large and small, a railroad spike, part of a muffler clamp, a rifle bullet, a piece of baling wire, a kitchen fork with most of its tines shiny and ground away. On the floor was a box of used wheel weights, bent gray molars of lead, and beside it the round tire balancer with its watery eyeball, a stationary black iris and a wandering pea-sized pupil. Coating the equipment, coating everything, was a fine grit of black rubber soot.

"Your main job is to watch the drive," Kirk said, nodding toward the pumps, "plus help me back here when you're not running gas. That and clean the johns."

In the afternoon Kirk took a phone call. He turned his back to me, murmured a few words into the receiver, then headed toward the door. "Furnace call," he said. Mr. Davies offered furnace service and repair along with heating oil. He also employed a third full-time man— Bud, the fuel-truck driver, whom I had not yet met.

"Furnace. In the summer?" I said.

Kirk stared at me briefly, then left. He squealed out in his blue Chevy, and I was alone at the station for the first time.

It was an overcast cool day. I discovered it was the

kind of weather that brought the tourists off the lakes and into town. Soon I had gas hoses running in four cars at once. I moved like a ballet dancer from car to car, throwing open hoods, pulling oil dipsticks, never forgetting a windshield, providing extra service, making perfect change.

When Kirk returned, he examined the till tape, scrutinized the gallons and the receipts, surveyed the front office. I pretended nonchalance. Bud, a potato-faced man in his late fifties who lived with his mother, arrived about the same time. He nodded a brief, almost shy hello to me.

"All well and good," Kirk said, "except somebody walked off with four No-Pest Strips." He gestured to the display box beside the cash registers. "When you're pumping gas you got to watch the damn till area or you're not gonna last here, Sutton."

Later, after Kirk was gone, Bud said, "Don't worry about it, kid. Kirk's having women trouble." Bud drew a mint toothpick from his shirt pocket, briefly counting the toothpicks remaining. He leaned on the counter to look out toward the street, toward the intersection. "Someday Kirk's gonna get his in a vise," Bud said. He rolled the toothpick from one side of his mouth to the other and stared at the stoplight that clicked as it changed from green to yellow. "Mark my words, in a vise."

That first short week, as Bud looked on, Kirk showed me the equipment of the back room. How to remove tires from rims on the pneumatic tire machine. How to fit new tires on rims. "With the tires as with the ladies, always use plenty of 'wienerschlider,' " Kirk said, pointing to the bucket of rubber lubricant. Bud rolled his eyes; I kept an even face. That week I learned the correct way to secure a wheel on a car's hub: one nut at a time in an alternating star-shaped pattern. This reduced the possibility of wheel imbalance. I learned the Shell approach to fixing large, split-rim truck tires: "Send them down the damn road," Kirk and Bud said in unison. They meant the co-op station at the edge of town, where most farmers (though not my father, and the others, who fixed their own) took their biggest tractor tires.

"I saw a split rim blow off once," Bud said, tonguing his toothpick to the opposite side of his mouth. "It took three fingers and the left ear off that . . . Benson kid? From that beef farm west of town?" He turned to Kirk for confirmation.

Kirk shrugged. "Way before my time."

"Anyway," Bud said, "she blew off right there." He pointed down to a pale, curving scar in the concrete.

And, that first week, I met the customers. I met a local man, sagged and frail Mr. Batson, who drove a Buick station wagon with two spare tires in the rear and two more tires strapped atop. "Would you check my spares, son?" he said. His breath was rank and coppery.

"Yes, sir." My little gauge sprang to forty-five pounds inflation. I checked it again. Thirty-two pounds was normal.

"Forty-five pounds?" he said.

I nodded.

"Let's bring them up to fifty," he said.

"Fifty, sir?" I said.

"You need plenty of air, son. You can never have too much air."

"Okay," I said.

Afterward I told Bud the hilarious story of the old man with four spare tires. "Weird," I said, "very weird."

Bud did not laugh. He lifted a hand sideways across his throat. "Cancer," he said. "The old guy is full of cancer up to here."

I met Stephen Knutson, the banker's son, and his 1964 Corvette Stingray. "Fill. Ethyl. And be careful of the paint," he said, not getting out of the car. He was a golden boy with John F. Kennedy hair and straight white teeth, and for years had dated Peggy Leikvold, the prettiest girl in his class. I knew that he recognized me from school—he was a senior last year and I was a freshman—but he did not acknowledge that fact. A duffel bag and a couple of tennis rackets were stashed behind the bucket seats.

"Taking a trip?" I said cheerfully as I washed the windshield; small talk was something Mr. Davies encouraged.

"What's it to you?" he said, looking at me for the first time.

He had undistinguished blue eyes. I shrugged and

finished his windshield in silence, then topped off the tank. "That'll be five dollars even."

"Charge it," he said, and drove off without signing. I went back to the till.

"Was that the Knutson kid?" Bud asked.

I nodded. "He didn't even sign for his gas."

"No problem," Bud said, and showed me how to write up a charge slip. "He's a real ass. It runs in his family."

I met Kirk's wife, Lynette, a thin-faced, dark-haired woman who wore cat's-eye glasses and was several years older than Kirk. She would have been pretty had she not plucked her eyebrows into black horseshoes. She drove a polished but rusted Ford station wagon with two kids in the back. "Is Kirk here?" she said, her eyes scanning the drive for his car or the wrecker. She had a whiny, suspicious voice.

"Kirk is engaged by a service call," I answered in my professional voice, which cracked only momentarily. I had been coached and I knew my lines: a service call—no more, no less, Kirk had said.

"Service call? Where?"

"Bud took the call, perhaps you could ask him?" Bud's face, visible at the window like a pale mushroom, now shrank away.

She glanced at the station, then at me. "Right," she said sarcastically, the corners of her mouth drawing downward. She gave me a final glare, then sped off.

Bud came out to the steps and stared after her car.

"That's Kirk's wife?" I said.

Bud rolled his toothpick. "Shotgun wedding."

I met a local housewife with blond hair piled high and sprayed in place. She seemed annoyed that I came out to wait on her, and she asked for fifty cents' worth of gas. She kept looking toward the office, the back room. "Isn't Kirk on today?" she finally said.

"Kirk is engaged by a service call."

"I'll bet he is," she said.

"Is there anything Bud or I might help you with?" I asked.

She gave me a long look. "Bud—it'd be a cold day in hell. And you—not for a couple of years."

My ears reddened like train semaphores.

"Unless you know furnaces, that is," she said, raising one eyebrow at me.

"No, ma'am," I stammered.

"There's the main boiler and then there's the pilot light," she said, gesturing, drawing a circle with her hands.

I nodded.

"Oh, you do know furnaces after all?"

"Well, kind of—I mean I know what a pilot light is," I stammered.

"Good. Good. A lot of men go through life never understanding the difference between a pilot light and the main boiler. My first husband, Bill, he never knew where to look. Matter of fact, he couldn't even find the basement."

I turned back to the station for help. Bud's pale face peered, unmoving, through the glass.

"Be sure to tell Kirk that Darlene's furnace needs its checkup, okay?"

For some reason I bowed, which tickled her fancy, and she drove off laughing. She made a sweeping, grandiose turn onto the highway—I held my breath as cars braked and swerved for her—and she proceeded untouched through the intersection.

"Son, you stay clear of that one," Bud said.

I met my first war protester. Kirk and I were under the hoist fastening a tailpipe to the belly of an Oldsmobile when a yellow-and-white Volkswagen bus pulled up to the far pumps. It had a camper-type top, New York plates, and a peace sign painted on the side. The rear of the bus was curtained.

"What we got here?" Bud said. We straightened up to look.

"Commie antiwar protesters," Kirk said.

"Sure as hell," Bud said.

We stared. Then I turned to head outside.

"Let 'em wait," Kirk commanded, reaching out for another muffler clamp. "They don't like it, they can get gas somewhere else."

We kept working. The yellow bus sat quietly in the drive. Several minutes passed. The driver, a bushy-

haired fellow with dark, round sunglasses, remained behind the wheel. After a while he got out and stretched;
face up to the sun, he held his arms wide and did a series
of calf-raises and squats. He was a skinny fellow, made
top-heavy by a large head, but he had excellent balance.

"A real weirdo," Bud said.

"Watch this," Kirk said. He headed into the drive.
Bud and I went to the doorway.

"How may we help you, *sir?*" Kirk said.

"Good day, brother. Five gallons regular." The man
nodded to Bud and me.

"By all means, *sir.*" Then the man turned his face
back to the sun, and Kirk winked at us.

"Check the oil, sir?"

"If you like, brother."

Kirk went to the rear and opened the lid. He lifted
the dipstick, returned it without inspection—then pretended to spot something beneath the engine. He went
back around to the sunning driver.

"I noticed your muffler bearings are loose, sir," he
said.

Beside me Bud's belly began to jiggle with silent
laughter.

"Muffler bearings?" the guy said.

"Yes, sir," Kirk said earnestly, "the muffler bearings.
They rotate the compression baffles inside the muffler.
When they're loose, your engine tends to overheat."

Bud's belly heaved with silent guffaws.

"Are you saying I need new muffler bearings, then?"

the man said, still facing the sun. "Or could these muffler bearings be fixed?"

"I could try to fix them," Kirk said. "Though it'd take a while."

"I see," the bushy-haired man said evenly. He turned and smiled at Kirk. "Then you could also fix my gravel pump?"

Kirk stared.

"And change my Goldwater fluid? Brother, brother—I may have long hair but I do all my own repairs."

Bud laughed audibly from the station doorway.

"Not that I'm being negative about you, brother," the man added, placing his hand on Kirk's shoulder.

"I'm not your damn brother," Kirk said, batting away his hand.

"We are all brothers," the man said, and headed to the bathroom.

While he was gone Kirk finished the gas. He looked over his shoulder to the closed men's room door, then suddenly bent low beneath the rear bumper of the van. Taking a small wrench from his pocket, he reached underneath, and moments later was standing up again wiping his hand on his pant leg. The man returned, paid for his gas, and then the yellow peace van headed west.

"What did you do to him?" Bud asked.

"Opened his oil plug a half turn," Kirk said, staring after the hippie van.

"Geez," Bud said.

" 'Brother, I do all my own repairs,' " Kirk mimicked. "Let's see him fix a fried engine about an hour down the road."

Bud nodded. Kirk grinned at me; I looked away.

"Somewhere out in the middle of nowhere—boom!" Kirk said.

"If the buzzards don't get him, the coyotes will," Bud said.

"Ought to send that kind to Vietnam," Kirk said, his grin fading as he stared after the yellow van. "That would teach him a lesson."

I met a beautiful woman in a blue Mercedes. Late in the afternoon, with Kirk gone on another furnace call, the bells rang twice—soft bells—well-spaced bells. I was fast learning their code: a single ring meant that a passing kid had stomped on the cord. Fast, loud bells meant a local tradesman—carpenter, roofer, plumber—always in a hurry and needing "just a squirt" of gas. Medium-paced bells meant the average tourist car. But slow bells meant a motor-home driver or else an old lady, both of whom entailed not seven-point service but seventy-times-seven.

Framed in the battered doorway of the back room, centered on a shiny white rectangle of pavement, sat the Mercedes. It was the small kind, a coupe. A woman drove. She wore sunglasses and a pale scarf tied at the chin. I hurried out.

"Good afternoon!" I said brightly. "Fill with ethyl?"

She didn't look up at me. "Fill. With ethyl," she murmured.

Her sunglasses were slightly pointy, with a narrow mother-of-pearl rim across the top. The lenses were deeply black, the kind I could not see through. I suddenly thought of Mr. Shell: surely there was no Mrs. Shell.

The car was dusty, bug-specked, and carried Virginia plates. The backseat contained a single large leather suitcase. I squatted behind the car to look for the gas cap and was rewarded. During my first week I had been stumped by a 1956 Chevy—the cap was behind the left taillight— and only yesterday by a 1959 Cadillac—high up in the right rear fin. To ask the driver was to have failed. When the pump whirred as its iron nozzle chilled in my hand and the sweet gasoline smell rose, I returned to the driver.

"Check your oil and water, ma'am?" I said. Why couldn't there be a Mrs. Shell?

"If you wish." Her voice was barely audible.

I went to the front of the blue Mercedes and searched for the hood latch, another test of professional competency. I ran my fingers over the grill, then under the bumper. I got down on my knees. I lay on my back. I went to the back room for a flashlight. I spent several minutes before the car, searching, feeling everywhere for the hood latch. Bud watched me through the station window. Finally I went around to the driver's side. "I'm sorry, ma'am," I said, my ears burning. "I can't seem to find the hood latch."

"Hood latch?" she murmured. She looked up at me for the first time. She had fine brown hair, an oval face with a thin, perfect nose. Her skin was clear and untanned.

"The oil," I said. "I was going to check your oil."

"Of course," she said—I had the feeling that behind her glasses she blinked; remembered where she was. "The hood latch is inside, down here somewhere." She opened her door and pointed down.

She wore a skirt, not a miniskirt but not long either, and she swung her legs to the side. I reached down, my tan arm alongside her white calf, and felt for the lever. "Got it," I said, and quickly stood up.

She didn't reply.

Behind the upraised hood I recovered my wits and found the dusty blue finger loop of the dipstick. It withdrew from the engine block long and brightly chromed, like a fine and drooping sword—but stained with black blood. I did not like the looks of that oil. Carefully I wiped the blade, inserted it, withdrew it again. Black, gritty oil hung well below the full line.

"You definitely need oil—at least two quarts!" I said, showing her the dipstick.

"Thank you," she murmured. She handed me her Shell credit card.

"Have you changed it recently?"

"It's my husband's car. He usually took care of those things. But he's not around now. He left me."

I was silent. Then I said, "Usually there's a sticker or a tag of some kind that tells when the oil was last changed. It's probably on the driver's door frame."

She shrugged.

I opened her door again and crouched to read the tag. Then I read the odometer. "It hasn't been changed in fifteen thousand miles!" I said.

"Is that bad?"

"Yes. Very. I could change it for you right now."

"No, thank you. Just put some in." Afterward, she signed for her gas, then looked around. "What town is this?"

"Hawk Bend. Minnesota," I added.

She watched a station wagon arrive at the far pumps. Some kids piled out and raced for the restrooms. She stared intently at them, then looked toward Main Street. I followed her gaze—and saw it through her eyes. One block of storefronts with painted tin awnings and fake fronts to modernize the red brick underneath. A bait shop. A clothing store. An ice cream store, open only in summer, with a candy-striped stagecoach on top. Elmo's Barbershop. A pool hall. One old general store, without awnings. A Woolworth's. Paula's Café. A bakery. Two hardware and two auto-parts stores. A lumberyard at the far end of town.

"What do people do here?" she asked.

"I dunno. Tourism, logging, farming, construction."

"And winters?"

"A lot of places close up. People just kind of get by," I said.

She turned to me. "And you?" She looked at my shirt, at the darker, blank oval where my mother had removed "Brian" (my own name badge was supposed to be here any day).

"Paul."

"Paul," she repeated.

"My folks have a dairy farm. I'm a sophomore in high school. Will be, that is," I bumbled on, though I had the feeling she wanted a different answer. "Three more years and I graduate."

"And then?"

"College, probably, though there's the draft. The war in Vietnam."

She nodded, then took another long look at Hawk Bend.

"Are there any nice girls here, one you could marry?"

"Yes, I suppose so," I stammered.

She looked far away down the highway. "That might be the best—marry someone you've known for a long time, someone you grew up with, then stay here, because the world out there is very overrated, Paul."

I was silent. Her blue Mercedes left the station, paused at the stoplight, then headed west.

I met an older man driving an immaculate 1953 Cadillac. He wore a pale silk shirt, pants pleated and wide-legged, and auburn leather shoes with pointed toes and a miniature brush on top. I had never seen clothes like that, not even in Kendrigan's. His shoes (they were right beside me as I ran gas in the big tank) stood out in particular: the tops of his loafers were a delicate leather mesh that squeaked softly when he moved, like expensive, oiled horse tack. He smelled of Old Spice and cigar smoke; of faraway places. My hands suddenly trembled on the pump handle: It was Mr. Shell.

"New on the job, son?" he said pleasantly.

Had he seen my sudden tremor? "Yes, sir."

He smiled.

I provided him the seven-point code, all the while looking for some way to give extra service. The cigar smell. Sure enough, a butt lay in the wide chrome ashtray. "Empty that ashtray for you, sir?"

"Why, thank you, son," he said, and stepped aside.

I not only emptied the butt, I buffed the ashtray.

"Good job, son. Name's Blomenfeld. Harry Blomenfeld. I've got a charge account here. My driver usually takes care of the car, but he's laid up today, so I'll sign the slip."

"Yes, sir," I said, hugely disappointed.

Later that afternoon, when Bud returned from a fuel oil delivery, he noticed the charge slip. "Kid Can was here!"

"Who?"

"Kid Can Blomenfeld."

"Who's he?"

"Right here. Here's his slip," Bud said, holding it up.

"Shouldn't I have let him charge?" I said quickly.

"No, no—he's good for it. He always pays cash at the end of every month," Bud said.

"So what about him?'

"What about him?" Bud said. "He's a big-time Chicago gangster. At least he was."

I looked down the highway; the Cadillac and soft-spoken Mr. Blomenfeld were long gone. "A gangster? Sure," I laughed.

At that moment Kirk came in.

"Paul waited on Harry Blomenfeld!" Bud said.

Kirk laughed loudly.

"Is there a joke?" I said.

"You, Sutton," Kirk said. "You're the joke."

"Everybody knows Kid Can," Bud explained. "He's got an estate out on Big Sandy Lake, high fences, body-guard, you name it."

"He seemed like just a nice old man," I said stubbornly.

"Nice?" Kirk said. "Nice? He once killed three men himself and had them run through a dog-food grinder. He went to trial but all the witnesses conveniently disappeared. Probably ended up as dog food, too. That's where he got the nickname—Kid Can."

I swallowed but held my ground. "Why would a gangster live in Hawk Bend, Minnesota?"

" 'Cause he can never go back to Chicago, stupid," Kirk said.

Toward week's end, I spoke for the first time to Stephen Knutson's girlfriend, Peggy Leikvold. Her father had a charge account at the station. As a senior at school that year, Peggy had been the glowing sun of the hallways. She pulled along an orbit of admirers, beginning, in closest ring, with the senior boys and ending with small, skinny fellows like myself who could only gaze from the far-off minor galaxy of tenth grade. She and Stephen Knutson were headed to the university in Minneapolis in the fall.

Today Peggy was alone. Peggy in her white sleeveless blouse.

"Hello. Fill with ethyl?" I said, trying to keep my gaze from slipping down her brown neck. I was successful, though I felt myself blush.

"Regular," she said, and leaned near the mirror to fluff up the dome of her short blond hair.

I hid out beneath the hood of the Ford Safari wagon, checking the oil and radiator, letting my blood subside, then came around to top off the tank. As she signed the gas ticket I gave in to temptation. Her tanned shoulders, the brown and downy rise of her breasts, the damp crescents under the arms of her sleeveless blouse—I stared shamelessly. Peggy Leikvold was a strong, athletic girl who was also valedictorian of her class. She was a girl who always seemed to be from somewhere else, not Hawk Bend.

"Have you seen Dale Bender?" she said suddenly, looking up at me.

"Dale Bender?" There was offense in my voice. Dale Bender was a fullback who had graduated, barely, the previous year. His family ran a logging and sawmill operation north of town.

"Yes, Dale Bender," she said impatiently.

"Sorry, no," I said.

She signed the charge slip and drove off.

On Friday, I met a white-haired nut-brown man driving a battered 1952 Oldsmobile with Nevada plates. He wanted ten gallons of gas in exchange for a belt buckle made of silver with bits of inlaid turquoise. I held the buckle in my hand; it was heavy and cool to the touch. I could see my father wearing it Christmas Day or on his birthday.

"Deal!" I said. I had enough money in my wallet to cover the gas.

The old man nodded wisely. He had a long thin braided ponytail. "It is a buckle of great power, my son," he said. "You must keep it in this protective box until you're ready to wear it or give it away." He took the buckle and placed it in a little box that had thick cotton inside; with a quick flourish of his hands he knotted string around the box. I checked his oil, finished the gas, then received my box and its buckle. As he drove away, I took the box inside.

"Hey, Bud, you have to see this belt buckle," I said, describing my prize as I untied the string. "I'm going to give it to my dad." Bud watched as I opened the box and unfolded the neat layers of cotton. Inside, at the bottom, was a single smooth gray stone.

I stared.

Kirk, just back from Elmo's with a fresh haircut, stepped forward to look. His new flattop smelled of butch wax. I whirled toward the door, looked west past the stoplight; the old man and his car were long gone.

"Nice buckle," Kirk said. "Except the belt loops are missing." He and Bud laughed until they had to wipe their eyes.

"Sorry, kid," Bud said.

That evening I told my mother about the belt buckle. She smiled; her blue eyes shone like the turquoise. "So, Paul," she said. "You've met the public."

3

Saturday on the farm I worked from dawn to dark. During the week I had kept up with feeding calves morning and night, but by week's end their pens were hardly "shipshape." I cleaned them with fork and shovel, then hauled the manure with tractor and spreader to the fallow west field. Jolting along in the sunshine and fresh warm breeze, I tried not to nod off, fall from the tractor, and run myself over.

Looking back, I saw a dust cloud rolling down our driveway; it was my father, off to town for baling twine and sickle parts. As his truck turned out of sight beyond the windbreak, my mother appeared in the garden with a hoe. She began work in the sweet corn—my job. I muttered something close to a curse and sped up the tractor. When I got back, almost thirty minutes later, the hoeing—two long rows—was half done.

"I thought you might need a little help," she said, her forehead glistening.

"I could have done it," I said. I found a second hoe.

She helped me a bit longer, then managed to be in the house when my father returned. Passing in the truck, he slowed to survey my garden work, then drove on.

By Sunday morning I had finally caught up with my

chores and wanted only to sleep—not sit through Church Meeting. But it was hard to avoid when it was held at my house.

In my religion, Sunday morning worship took place in the home. Our home, since we had the largest living room. As I began to set up folding chairs, tires scraped on gravel. My mother looked out the window and sighed. "Mrs. Halgrimson. Already." It was barely nine-twenty a.m. Worship started at ten.

"Hungry for the word of God," my father remarked from his reading chair. He lowered his Bible. "Go help her in, son."

I muttered something and went outside. The smaller problem with having Church Meeting at our house was that the Elders like Mrs. Halgrimson often drove onto the lawn or backed over my mother's iris beds. The larger problem was trying to explain to other kids why I didn't go to a "real" church. "Come on, Sutton, how can a religion have no name *and* no church?"

During the school year my inquisition took place every Wednesday morning right after "release time." Release time was for town kids who went to local churches, to their Bible school and various confirmation classes; they got to leave school while Richard Silver (the only Jewish kid in town), Ricky Holds Eagle, and I remained at our desks for "independent reading." My classmates returned, two hours later, full of religion and candy—their lips were green, their tongues fiery red.

"Come on, Sutton—why don't you go to church?"

"Yeah, ain't you a Christian?" they'd sneer, beginning to look at Richard and Ricky as well. Richard pasted a weird smile on his face and pretended to read; Ricky's face went blank as tree bark.

"I am a Christian," I'd say, "but my religion is non-denominational."

"What the hell does that mean?"

"It means it has no name."

"How can a religion have no name?!"

As a matter of pride I did not repeat myself.

"So where's your stupid church then?"

"I told you, in our home."

"You're weird, Sutton."

This Sunday morning Mrs. Halgrimson's face homed in on mine. "So, Paul, I heard you're working in town."

"That's right," I said. I pretended to tighten one of the nuts on her aluminum walker.

"How's your father supposed to manage here at home?" She paused. Her blue, rheumy eyes bored into mine.

"We'll make do," I said.

"I hope you're not expecting the other boys to do your work?"

"No, Mrs. Halgrimson."

"Well, how much do they pay you in town?" she continued as we stumped our way along.

"One-fifty an hour."

"You'll probably start smoking, too," she said.

"I hope not, Mrs. Halgrimson," I said. "My faith will be tested, but I know you'll be praying for me."

"Hummmmph," she said, and I braced for the front steps.

Gradually, the others arrived.

George Stephens, an older farmer who had a crushed, stiff leg, was hard of hearing, and could be counted on, during testimony, to speak of the hardship of Abraham.

Mattie Swenson, a round-faced elementary-school teacher and her husband, Ray, a mechanic. While most in the Faith were rural people, a few—those on the fringes of town life, or who were "different"—came from Hawk Bend. Ray Swenson was not actually, physically there. Ray remained in their car during Meeting, rain or shine or twenty below, slouched behind the wheel, chain-smoking cigarettes, then flipping butts onto the lawn. It was my job, afterward, to trot out to the car and invite Ray into the house for coffee and a bite to eat. Hungry by then, he usually came in from the cold. Many a prayer was directed toward softening Ray Swenson's hard heart, and a chair was always left empty beside Mattie—just in case.

Hulking Helmer Klemke with his battered face and raspy voice. He had been a gandy dancer with Northern Pacific Railroad, had taken whores and drunk whiskey and boxed bare-knuckled from Michigan to Seattle, bottoming out in the Depression work camps before seeing the Light. Helmer had a tendency to weep during testimony, his and others', and then honk his nose onto his sleeve. My mother kept a box of Kleenex near his chair.

William Crews, a young accountant from town whose wife was an Avon representative and always on the road, sometimes for days at a time. He was a pale, serious man who trembled during his testimony, which often contained allusions to Jezebel.

The VandenEides, who milked seventy Brown Swiss and whose five daughters each had braids and noses both as thick as haymow ropes, and had about them a faint smell of oak bark, a scent that did odd things to my heart rate.

The Grundlags, the only family who raised hogs, and who smelled like it.

The Sorheims, who milked eighty Holsteins, and whose twin sons, Gus and Hans, were two years older than me and fifty pounds more muscled. When we hayed together they took pride in tossing sixty-pound bales, one in each hand, and smirked at me, who couldn't. However, on Sundays, I took pleasure in their brief, stammering testimonies; at the sudden blotchy color on their necks; at words that came out thick and heavy as potatoes.

Not that I could do any better (actually I was sure I could), but I had never tried. Ours was a religion where baptism came not at birth but "of age." "Like Jews!" Richard Silver had said when once during release time we shared our sad stories. "Sort of," I replied; I certainly didn't need him as my new best friend. Anyway, at nearly sixteen I was now of age and then some; it was expected that, during Church Convention at summer's end, I would "profess"—that is, declare my faith, and be baptized in the river.

Washed of my sins.

Set free.

But set free of what? That was the question. And the kind with which I drove the Workers crazy during our Bible study conversations. Frankly, I hadn't heard the call, but it couldn't be that hard to fake. Today, for example, I could have spoken to Matthew, chapter 7: how this very week I had unfairly judged a man. I would tell the story of Mr. Batson and his greatly inflated spare tires, his need for faith near the hour of death. I could take the metaphor of tires and roll with it. Tires were like people; the constant wear on their rubber bodies inevitably wore them down, two-ply tires around the twenty-thousand-mile mark and four-plies around forty thousand, unless of course they were steel-belted radials. And the air inside tires was like faith in the Lord, which kept people pumped up with the spirit of God . . .

I felt a sharp tap on my shin. My father was looking sternly at me. I straightened in my chair, wiped drool from my chin. I had fallen asleep.

During communion the cup of Welch's grape juice came around. I passed it on. Following the cup came the bread, one slice from which, in the old style, each person of age pinched off his or her portion. This body of Christ in Wonder bread did not crumble as much as homemade, my mother had found. As I watched it pass down the line, its soft, curving whiteness filled me with a vision of Peggy Leikvold's full white sleeveless blouse. I let my eyes drift shut in order to see her better. She began to arrive at the station in smaller and smaller blouses, and the last ones were made of brown chamois, the same velvety material that I used to buff and polish her windshield while she smiled at me from below . . . My father's sharp kick jolted me again. I quickly put my hymn book over my lap and straightened up for the final song. Blessedly, someone had chosen 311, the shortest in the hymnal.

After Meeting, most of the Friends stayed, as usual, for coffee. Another annoyance. I was always starving to death at this point. One of the older VandenEide girls— Mary, I think—came up to me and whispered, "So it's true, you're working in town!"

"Yes," I said.

"What are the Workers going to say?" she said.

"Who cares?" I said, and pretended nonchalance. She giggled and fled back to her covey of sisters. The Workers' circuit brought them to our congregation on the last Sunday of each month—but that was a whole three weeks off.

Gus Sorheim jostled me from the cinnamon-roll line. "When haying time comes, my dad said we ain't gonna do your share of the work," he whispered hoarsely.

"We ain't," his brother, Hans, added, bumping me from the other side.

I stared at them, at their beetle brows, their small

heads perched on gigantic shoulders. "So? I heard you both have to take summer school in order to graduate."

They glared at me. "So?" Gus said.

"Yeah, so?" Hans added.

"So what's the difference between me working in town and you going to summer school?"

Their eyes glazed and narrowed.

"It's different," Gus said.

"Yeah, it's different," Hans added.

After everyone had finally cleared out, and as I put away the folding chairs, I felt suddenly and crushingly sad. But maybe I was just hungry.

4

Monday afternoon the Workers found me. I came around the gas pumps to the window of an older Chevy sedan, and it was them, two tidy, clean-shaven men. Workers always came in pairs; sometimes they were called "two by twos" (Mark 6:7) by people not in the Faith. This pair, one younger, one older, was Jeff Hillman and Garland Brown. Both wore short-sleeved white shirts and narrow black ties.

"Hello, Paul," they said together.

"Ah . . . hullo!" I said. I suddenly felt like I was guilty of something. The two preachers' car was a loaner from someone in the Faith, as Workers had no possessions ("Provide neither gold, nor silver, nor brass in your purses, nor scrip for your journey, neither two coats, neither shoes." Matthew 10:9–10). They also never married, which always seemed a little weird to me.

"We heard you were working in town this summer," Jeff said.

I swallowed. "That's true."

"We're passing through to the north and wanted to say hello," Garland added.

"Yes, thank you," I said, still fumbling. "Ah, fill with ethyl?"

"Oh no," Jeff said, glancing at the prices on the pump, "just a couple dollars of regular." They got out to stretch and look around. I ran the gas. They were pale men with high foreheads and white arms. Garland began to wash the windshield.

"I'll do that," I called.

"Oh no, a little real work is good for me," he said.

They laughed pleasantly at their joke.

I finished the gas.

"Thank you, Paul," they said. They made no move to pay.

"I'll cover it," I said. "It's only two bucks."

"No, of course not," Jeff said. "Free gas is certainly not why we came." He fished two dollars from a thin wallet.

"We came to see you, Paul," Garland said.

"Thank you," I said.

There was silence. "Have you been keeping up with your Bible reading?" Jeff asked.

"Yes," I said. I felt my Adam's apple bob.

"Good. Good to hear, Paul."

"We'll be wanting to go over the assigned chapters with you soon," Garland said.

"I'll be ready," I replied.

"Convention is less than three months away," Jeff said.

I nodded. Behind me, bells rang as another car arrived at the pumps.

Garland said, "What a great day it will be, Paul,

when you walk up that aisle and accept Jesus Christ as your Lord and savior."

"Thank you," I said stupidly. The stoplight clicked loudly.

Another car pulled up, and then one behind it; by now Bud was looking out the window.

"Shall we have a brief prayer and then be on our way?" Garland said.

"Ah . . . okay," I said. I glanced about.

The two men bowed their heads and so did I. Garland Brown led a brief prayer ending with, "So thank you, Lord, for granting Paul this opportunity to test himself in the world of fire and sin. Amen."

We shook hands and then they slowly drove away. I hurried to my customers. As I came into the office, Bud said, "Who in the heck were those guys?"

5

On Thursday a logging truck pulled up to the rear of the station. The battered Kenworth tractor, its trailer loaded with a tall rick of logs, groaned to a halt. Dust and the scent of freshly cut spruce tumbled forward into the service bay. Kirk, Bud, and I stared. The Kenworth's tires looked fully inflated, had no flapping recaps; no steam or leaks issued from beneath the hood.

"Send him down the damn road," Bud muttered nonetheless. "We don't work on logging trucks, and sure as hell not loaded ones."

"Go get 'em, Pauly," Kirk said, and turned again to his work on a carburetor.

I stepped outside in the sunlight as the truck's engine died. The sweet, pitchy smell of spruce was stronger than the little green Pine Tree Aire Fresheners we sold up front.

BENDER AND SONS the truck door read, its letters furred with oil and fine sawdust. Dale Bender himself swung down from the cab. At almost five feet ten I was the same height as Dale, but there comparisons stopped. He had black Elvis hair; mine was curly yellow. He had a rectangular, lantern jaw; I had a penlight. His shoulders, confined by a smudged white T-shirt, were as square and wide as a plow; mine were as narrow and bony as a silage fork. His biceps, stitched with veins, were softballs; mine were tennis balls at best. Tucked up in his left shirt-sleeve, making him still wider, was a pack of cigarettes. As I approached, he unrolled his sleeve, shook a Lucky Strike from the pack, and lit it. He used a stick match, flicking off the head with a thumbnail and bending his dark hair to the flame, then looking up and shaking out the match all in one extended gesture. Dale leaned against his truck. "What say, Sutton?"

As he exhaled, I breathed in his smoke. Dale Bender knew my name; not only that, he had spoken it with the comradely tone of one country boy to another.

"How's it going, Dale?"

"It's got to go," he said, and spit.

His words struck me as truly wise. But maybe that was because, at school last year, I could not recall Dale Bender saying anything. Ever. Not one word. To most kids, high school was life at its most dramatic; for Dale, high school had been an annoyance. He plodded through the halls, the cafeteria line, like a prisoner whose life was on hold. His only pleasure came in football, where as a tackle he crushed ball carriers, and in wrestling, where he pinned his opponents quickly and violently, often injuring them.

"You seen Peggy Leikvold?"

"Peggy Leikvold?"

"You deaf? Your hearing aid need batteries?"

"No," I fumbled. "I mean, no I haven't seen her today."

"When did you see her?"

"Last week."

"When last week?"

"Midweek, I guess. Wednesday. Thursday."

"You guess, Sutton?"

I swallowed. "She charged gas. I could check the slips."

Dale smiled and tilted back his head for a long draw on his cigarette. I realized he was kidding. I let out a breath. Then he narrowed his eyes. "She ask about me?"

I nodded yes.

"What did she say?"

"She said, 'Have you seen Dale Bender?' "

"That's it?"

"Word for word."

"Was she with that creep Knutson?"

"No."

"That's 'cause he's out of town."

"When I filled his Corvette, Knutson did have a suitcase," I offered.

"Tennis camp," Dale said, and spit again. "Two weeks at some fancy-ass tennis camp. Must be nice." He drew on his Lucky Strike, looked toward the intersection, and exhaled a long contrail of smoke. "Anyway, Sutton, I want you to give Peggy a message."

I waited.

He turned. "Tell her I asked if she asked about me."

I nodded.

"Got it, Sutton?"

"Got it," I said.

"Say it," he said.

I repeated it.

"That's it," Dale said, taking a last draw, then flicking his cigarette into the street. He climbed into the cab, then leaned out his window. "One more thing."

I waited.

"I want you to keep an eye out for Peggy."

"An eye out?"

"I want to know when she comes in, I want to know what she says."

"Okay," I said.

"She drives by, I want to know who she's with."

"I'll try. It gets busy," I said.

He pointed his finger at me and raised one eyebrow. "Try hard, Sutton." Then his truck engine revved. Slowly he eased backward onto the street, after which, gear by gear, with heavy double-clutch shifting, the truck rumbled away north. He was still shifting, in no hurry, as one cannot be with his kind of load, when the Kenworth rolled out of sight.

Inside the office, Kirk said, "What did Bender want?"

"Peggy Leikvold."

"Peggy Leikvold?" He laughed. "Just 'cause he got his draft notice doesn't mean he gets Peggy Leikvold."

"Dale got drafted?" I said quickly.

"Shipping out sometime this summer," Bud said. "Be in Vietnam by fall."

We were all silent.

"Maybe girls like that sort of thing," Kirk said. He stared at the traffic. "Guys who might not be coming back."

"If anybody comes back from Vietnam, it'll be Dale," I said.

Kirk turned to me. "What would you or any of your family know about it, Sutton?"

6

Saturday dawned red, hot, and dewless. At the breakfast table my father gave thanks for a perfect haying day—when the phone rang. He continued, unhurried, with the blessing. My mother and I peeked at each other. After he said "Amen," my mother snatched up the receiver on the tenth ring.

"It's Mr. Davies. At the station," my mother said. She frowned and held out the receiver to me.

I listened, then covered the receiver. My father passed the oatmeal bowl in silence; my mother waited for me to speak.

"They're shorthanded," I said. "Mr. Davies wanted to know if I could come in."

"Surely not today?" my father said. His eyes flickered to the dry blue skies outside.

"Sorry," I said.

My father poured cream onto his cereal. Stirred in a spoonful of brown sugar. Silence towered.

"What should I tell him?" I murmured.

"Tell him you'll call back in just a few minutes," my mother said.

I spoke into the phone.

"All right, but I need you, Sutton," Mr. Davies

replied. "Something with Kirk, his wife or what not, so he can't make it. Also, it would be time and a half for you on Saturdays."

"Yes, sir. Give me a couple of minutes." I hung up.

We all looked at each other.

"The others are coming with the baler, right?" my mother asked.

My father nodded. "The Sorheim boys, a whole crew. It's our turn to hay today."

"What if we got someone to take Paul's place on the wagon?"

"Everybody in the county will be baling hay today," my father said.

My mother ignored the last part. "The Jenson boy?" she said. "He's old enough to throw bales."

"Worthless," my father said.

"How about his brother? That younger one."

"He's eight years old, nine at the most."

"Can he lift a hay bale? That's all that counts, right?" my mother said.

A fine vein began to pulse in my father's cheek. "He's too young. He won't be able to keep up."

"How about George Lehman's boy, that slow one?" my mother ventured.

"Donny Lehman?" my father said, his voice dipping ominously. "The last time Donny Lehman worked for someone, he fell asleep on the wagon, rolled off, and was nearly run over."

There was silence in the kitchen. I looked at the clock: already three minutes had passed.

"I'll check around in town," my mother said evenly. "At the school. It'll be open Saturday morning. Sometimes at the high school they have a list of kids who want to work."

"Town kids, Donny Lehman. God's hooks!" my father thundered. "I'm trying to put up hay, not start a circus." As he left the house the screen door slammed so hard the dishes rattled.

My mother turned to me. She swallowed. "Call Mr. Davies back. Tell him you'll be there."

"No. I'll tell him I can't come. I'll quit. It's all right."

"No, you won't quit," she said quickly. "Don't fret, Paul. I'll think of something. Now let's go or you'll be late for work."

I hurriedly changed into my uniform. As my mother and I were leaving, there was already dust from a small convoy of pickups and wagons, along with two tractors and the all-important hay baler. It was my luck to meet the others at the entrance to the highway.

I stopped the truck. Gus Sorheim leaned out his window and looked down at me. "Where you think you're going?"

"Town," I said.

His eyes went to my Shell shirt, my bow tie.

"Paul has to work today," my mother added.

"I told you—we ain't gonna do your work for you," Gus said, ignoring her.

· 58 ·

"Yeah," echoed Hans from another tractor.

Their father, Herman Sorheim, narrowed his eyes. "You got somebody to take your place, Paul?"

"Not yet," I said.

"We'll find someone," my mother said.

The men, about a half dozen all together, all in straw hats, looked at each other. Walter VandenEide cleared his throat. "We've talked among ourselves about this," he said apologetically. "We think Paul is setting a bad example for the other boys in the Faith."

"Or maybe a good example," my mother said.

"And how would that be?"

"We need to make sure our sons—and daughters—know more than farm life. It's 1965. The world is changing before our eyes."

"Not for the better," Walter VandenEide said.

"That's right," Herman Sorheim added.

Gus and Hans glanced at each other, then said in unison, "Yeah, that's right."

There was silence. Herman Sorheim turned, for the first time, and spoke directly to my mother. "I'm sorry, Sarah."

"Sorry? For what?" my mother said. She got out of the truck and came around to the tractor tire (she was tiny beside it), looking up at the men.

Herman cleared his throat. "Unless Paul does his fair share of work, we're going to have to move on to the next farm."

Somewhere in the silence, a crow cawed.

"But it's our turn for the baler, right?" my mother said. "We always come right after you, yes, Walter?"

"Yes," Walter allowed.

"So if you're going to move on, park the baler and the wagons. We'll manage ourselves," my mother said.

The men in straw hats looked at each other. There was murmuring, some of it angry. Then they dismounted, unhooked the baler and wagons, and left.

My mother and I watched them go. She looked back toward our house. "Oh, Paul," she said, "what have I done?"

By then my father was walking quickly down the driveway. My mother hesitated, then walked forward to meet him halfway. As I watched them draw close my heartbeat began to boom. Out of my earshot, Mother talked to him. With gestures. He took off his straw hat and looked at the ground as he listened. Then he stared down the road at the dust of the others, who were out of sight by now. Suddenly my father threw down his hat and raised his arm as if to strike her. My mother braced for a blow but did not turn away. The back of my father's hand hung in the air like a bird—a dark hawk—then slowly lowered itself. When it was fully down, my mother walked away, and my father dropped to his knees in the road, and bowed his head. He did not look at us as we drove away.

I arrived much to the relief of Mr. Davies, who was manning the pumps himself, clumsily running gas. As I exited the pickup, my mother said suddenly, "Paul, I think I know how to get that hay baled." Her eyes were shiny again.

"How?" I said quickly.

"You'll see," she said, and off she drove with a chirp of the tires.

A half hour later I was on the driveway "sticking" the underground tanks with the tall measuring rod, then marking gasoline levels on my clipboard (the most managerial of my duties), when my mother drove back through the intersection. In the rear of the pickup rode four men. Two of them were Indian. The wind flapped their long gleaming ponytails. The other two were white men who had turned their very pale mugs into the sunlight, which it appeared they had not seen for some time. Following the pickup was the deputy sheriff's car.

My mother tooted the horn and waved at me as she drove through the intersection on yellow.

Bud came out on the station steps. "Wasn't that your ma?"

"Yes," I said, looking after the truck.

"Looks like she had a truckload of jailbirds."

At ten o'clock I called home to see how things were going. There was no answer.

At noon I called home again. My mother answered.

"Who were those guys in the pickup?" I asked immediately.

"Hay help," she said. "Harvey, Darrell, Clyde, and Dave."

"Is everything okay?" I said.

"Very okay," she said easily. There were voices in the background, and the loud clink of silverware on plates. She seemed busy.

"Listen, I can't get off work until five," I said.

"No problem, things are going fine," my mother said. "Why wouldn't they be?"

"Just checking," I said.

"You were worried?" my mother said.

"No," I said.

"Sure you weren't." She laughed and hung up.

That afternoon the pumps and driveway baked in the heat, and business was fairly steady, but the clock hands inched as slowly as a wood tick up my leg. I called again. No answer. I paced. I checked the clock. I imagined my parents tied up, the barn burned, the pickup stolen.

At five my mother had not arrived to pick me up. Earlier I had called but got no answer. However, I couldn't leave in any case. Tim, who had the late shift, finally pulled in at five-ten, emerging from his battered Ford Falcon. He was a round-shouldered, wiry guy with a wispy black mustache, and he leaned low to give his wife a kiss. Her face was wide and pimpled (like the rest of her, I imagined) and their two kids howled in the backseat. After a glance and a wink to me, Tim gave his wife, as usual, a quick squeeze on her breast.

"Tim!" she cried as usual, looking toward me with her milky, gap-toothed grin.

I looked away, at the clock.

"You ought to get married," Tim said to me as his wife drove off.

"Then I could have it anytime," I replied, beating him to his own line.

"Anytime!" he said, winking, waggling his eyebrows. He was a guy who liked predictable exchanges. Me, I just wanted to go home.

After my mother finally arrived, she would tell me nothing about the day's work. "You'll see," she said. As we came in view of the farm, the nearest hayfield was empty but for a faint mesh of wagon trails across the pale stubble. Tractor exhaust and baler dust rose from the second, larger field, which itself was two-thirds done.

"Jesus!" I said.

"Who may be found in the New Testament!" my mother replied sharply.

"Sorry!" Swearing had become part of my life.

On the wagon, seven bales high, a brown-skinned man stood straight and sharp as a hood ornament. Below him a big-bellied white guy tossed bales upward like a baggage handler throwing little green suitcases. Closer in, below the broad face of the barn, sat the small tractor and a near-empty wagon. The second Indian man stood on it beside the hay elevator, the skinny, ladderlike conveyor which was filled with a line of bales moving steadily into the loft. The Indian man chewed slowly on a piece of hay as he watched our pickup drive in. He did not appear to be sweating.

I hopped out and trotted into the field.

"Hello!" I called out to my father, who waved briefly but did not slow the tractor.

I caught up, vaulted aboard.

"How many bales?" I shouted into his ear.

"Twelve hundred and counting," he called out. He glanced back to the pair on the wagon.

"I'll help you finish," I said.

"No need," he said, not looking at me. "Why don't you go and help your mother."

At supper my mother had the men wash up in the summer sink on the porch. Their sweat smelled liquory, like Mr. Davies, but stronger, ranker.

"Boil it out of you, hey?" said Darrell, one of the Indian men, bending to run water over his head, slicking back his plum-colored hair.

Harvey, the thicker of the white guys, sighed in agreement and wiped his pink face. "Sweat is a waste of perfectly good liquor," he said, still panting. "Whose idea was this anyway?"

"Hers," the second Indian man, Clyde, said as he pointed to my mother.

"That's right," she said, setting the first of three great frying pans of Swiss steak onto the table. "There's no sense good men sitting in jail when you could be out in the fresh air earning a square dollar."

"Perhaps," Harvey said, tugging once at his throat

then looking to the refrigerator, "but a cold beverage of some kind—if there was such a thing in this house—might finally convince me."

My mother eyed him.

"He means a beer," Darrell said.

The men guffawed. Just then Father came onto the porch and took off his gloves.

"A beverage is what I said," Harvey continued, "though that would include, yes indeed, one of the malted or barley variety." He looked hopefully at my mother.

"This is a religious family," my father said, purposefully looking my way. "In this house it's water, lemonade, milk, tea, or coffee. If you men would stick to those beverages, you wouldn't end up in trouble like you have."

There was silence. Harvey frowned. Silent battered Dave looked down. Darrell and Clyde looked sideways at each other.

"You men sit in your same spots as dinnertime," my mother said quickly. "We'll soon be eating."

The four clattered their chairs and took their places. Seated, Dave reached immediately for the steaming bowl of potatoes, then drew back his hands at Harvey's stern look. "Thank you, Harvey," Mother said. She waited for my father to take his seat and give the blessing.

As my father prayed, I opened my eyes to watch the four men. Three of them surveyed the food; hangdog Dave watched my father. As the blessing continued, Dave's nose started to twitch and twist; tears began to leak from his eyes. His long turkey neck pulsed up and down at the throat, and just as my father said "Amen," Dave broke out into deep, chest-heaving sobs.

Mother got up without a word, went to the kitchen sink, and brought back a cool wet washcloth. There, before all of us, she carefully wiped Dave's battered alcoholic face, his big red nose, his beak chin. "My folks, they were good people," Dave blubbered.

"You're going to be all right," she said to him quietly.

"I don't know what happened to me," he said. "Where I went wrong."

"You need to eat something. Once you do, the world will look different," my mother said.

Snuffling, Dave did, and slowly, it must have. Conversation gradually returned. My father, for his part, asked each man what he'd done to land in jail.

"Borrowing gas," Darrell said.

"Third-degree assault," Clyde said.

"Habitual drunkenness," Dave whispered.

"A misunderstanding at the bank," Harvey answered.

"And at the hardware store and the gas station," Clyde said. The two men grinned widely; even Dave smiled a little.

"The art of making change is clearly lost on people nowadays," Harvey said indignantly. "I was passing through town and wanted only some twenties for my hundred dollar bill—a simple enough transaction."

"And then he wanted tens for his twenties or was it fives for his tens?" Darrell said.

"Actually it was tens for my fives," Harvey answered.

There was laughter around the table. My mother clucked her tongue but couldn't hold back a smile. Soon it was time for pie and coffee.

"Sure beats that mud they give you in town," Clyde said, holding up his cup.

"The coffee at the jail is horse piss!" Dave exclaimed. His eyes widened as he glanced at my mother; he touched a hand to his mouth. His eyes brimmed with tears again.

"More pie?" my mother said to him.

He nodded.

"How much longer you fellows in the brig?" my father asked.

Around the circle of the table, the men counted off. "Fifty-one days." "Thirty-two." "Forty-seven." "Twelve."

That was Dave.

"Why, that's less than two weeks," my mother said to Dave encouragingly.

Dave shrugged.

"So what are your plans when you get out?" my mother asked. She poured more coffee.

"I dunno," Dave said. "Head west maybe. Put out my thumb and see where it takes me."

My mother glanced at my father, then at me, then back to Dave.

The men finished, eating more than any four men I had ever seen, emptying every frying pan, every bowl, shining the bottoms of their plates with sops of bread, then killing off a rhubarb pie and an apple pie—eating until there was the sound of a car in the yard. Clyde and Darrell swiveled their heads to listen. A car door slammed.

There was a jingling sound, then a sharp rapping on the door. Silhouetted on the porch steps was the deputy sheriff, his holstered gun a dark tumor on his hip.

Half out of their chairs, Clyde and Darrell looked toward the kitchen window—to its thin screen, the grove, then the open fields beyond.

"Don't," Harvey said.

There was a long, frozen moment. Then Clyde let out a breath and settled back into his chair. Darrell followed suit.

My father rose and showed in the deputy, Lance Dickinson, a thick man, not old, with a sharp flattop.

"So," the deputy said loudly to my father, "how did these boys work out for you?"

"These men did fine," my mother said.

"Well then, it's time to saddle up, boys," the deputy said. His webbed belt was laden with shiny dangling cuffs, a whistle, the nickel-plated gun, the butt of a nightstick. "Back to the ranch before sundown, that was the deal, boys."

"We ain't done with our coffee," Clyde said.

There was a moment of silence in the kitchen. Darrell and Clyde would not look at the deputy.

"Well, there's a coffee machine at home, ain't there, boys!" the deputy said sharply. He stepped forward and clapped Clyde hard on the back. "Now shake a leg."

The four men drained their cups ever so slowly, then rose from the table.

"Thanks again, ma'am," Dave said.

"You're welcome, Dave. Anytime," she said.

"Let's go," the deputy said, steering Dave along.

"They're fine workers," my mother said as Clyde, Darrell, Harvey, and Dave were herded onto the porch.

"And model citizens, too, right, boys?" the deputy said, laughing at his joke.

The prisoners said nothing. On the porch my father paid the men, after which the deputy drove them away.

Then it was just the three of us, alone in the kitchen with the smeared plates and cooling pans. We set about washing the dishes—my father helped as well—but the house felt smaller, quiet, empty.

7

After my last round of chores that night, I went into our little front room to catch up on my Bible reading. My legs and feet ached, my hands were oil-stained beyond soap, my fingernails chipped, my eyelids heavy. I fell onto the couch, but didn't allow myself to stretch out.

I looked at this week's assigned readings from the Workers: the book of Judges. I sighed. I gave it five minutes. The story of Samson was always interesting, but enough with the misery of Israel. I flipped forward to Proverbs. Even though it basically stated right up front "The Object of the Book: To Warn the Young," at least it had some good advice. The proverbs were essentially a father nagging a son about the right way to live, but for some reason I never minded them. Plus they were short.

I paged along tiredly, looking for a proverb to catch my attention. I didn't have to worry about being slothful. Contentious, angry, and impatient—yes. Obedient— mostly yes. Lustful—I thought hourly of Peggy Leikvold. Unchaste—no, I didn't even have a girlfriend. Tale-bearing—no. Charitable—yes, I needed to be nicer to my parents. Bearing false witness—sometimes, though up to now in fairly minor ways. Still, according to most of the proverbs, I was not the worst person in the world.

Which made me wonder how real sinners—an odd-and-sod like Dave the jailbird, for example—might feel when they read the Bible, and the Old Testament in particular.

The New Testament at least tended to give people a second chance. I tipped back on the couch and thought about things. I wondered who I would marry. Peggy Leikvold was three years older, which was a lot in high school, but diminished with age. Between, say, the ages of sixty-five and sixty-two, three years was no big deal. I imagined us raising a family, growing old in Hawk Bend . . .

"Paul," my father said. "Paul!" He jerked my arm.

"What!?" I sat up quickly, smacked my lips. There was a wet spot on the couch cushion where my mouth had been. I glanced at my Bible, which had slipped onto the floor. The light had changed in the windows; it was dark now, well after sundown. "Sorry."

"Did you finish your reading?" he asked, raising one bushy eyebrow. He picked up the sheet of assigned chapters, which also lay on the floor.

"Kind of," I said.

He pursed his lips. His eyes were stern. "You'd better go to bed, get some sleep, then try again tomorrow."

"Yes, Father," I said. I got out of there before he quizzed me on Gideon, Mideon, and the Ammonite invasion.

8

Sunday after Meeting I rested. Make that slept—like a dead man. I slept and slept and, when I got up, ate hugely, ravenously. My mother had a worried look about her as she watched me eat.

"You must be growing," she said.

That night I heard them murmuring, late, in their bedroom. I was not sleepy since I'd napped so much, and so I laid out my pressed and starched uniform for Monday, then tried to read my Bible—with no success. I lay there in the dark well past midnight listening to WLS out of Chicago. At low volume the Rolling Stones, the Beach Boys, and the Byrds whispered under my blankets.

On Monday, when my mother picked me up after work, she was smiling.

"What's up?" I said cautiously.

"You'll see," she said.

At home, someone—not my father, certainly—was in the garden hoeing. "Dave the Jailbird!"

"Don't call him that," my mother said.

Dave waved, then leaned on his hoe to watch us pass, as if he'd never seen a 1958 Ford pickup.

"How long has he been here?" I said. For some reason I was annoyed.

"Most of the day. With a hoe he's not nearly as good as you, but he'll do for now," my mother said.

"Is he out of jail? I thought he had a couple of weeks left."

"He does. But I talked to the sheriff, and he allowed Dave a day pass to work out here."

"For just today?"

"No. Every day. Until his term is finished." She parked the truck.

"I was keeping up," I said crabbily as I got out. I stared back at the garden. He was using my personal long-handled hoe, the one I kept razor sharp.

"Yes and no," my mother said. "He's also taken care of the calf pens. Your father and I thought that might be helpful to you. So you're not quite so tired in the evenings." She raised one eyebrow and gave me a good look.

"We have to pay him, right?"

"Yes. But not a lot."

"I'll chip in," I said begrudgingly. Now I was more than annoyed; I'd been counting my hours, figuring my wages with an eye toward an eight-track-tape player for the truck. In two weeks I'd have my license.

"Thank you. We'll work out the details later. Right now the sheriff's happy, Dave's happy—and I hope you are, too." She cocked her head as she looked at me.

I manufactured a smile. "Sure," I said.

"Dave!" my mother called. "Suppertime." Dave tossed my hoe in the weeds and was on his way to eat before it hit the ground.

At the table Dave sat down—in my place.

My mother's eyes flickered to me. "Ah, Dave? Would you mind sitting one place to the right? That's where Paul usually sits."

"It's no problem, Dave," I said.

"All right," Dave said easily, and didn't move.

More annoyance.

To begin the meal, Dave bowed his long, battered face, scrunched up his eyes, and concentrated. I smiled; my mother glared at me. After my father finished grace, Dave leaned toward my father and with great earnestness, said, "Thank you, sir. Thank you so much!"

My mother rapped my shin with her foot.

"You're quite welcome, Dave," my father said, with a glance toward me. "Shall we eat?"

But Dave was already reaching for the steaming bowl of mashed potatoes. There was sweet corn also.

"Would you pass the corn along?" my mother asked Dave.

"Sure," Dave mumbled through a full mouth. He reached for a yellow ear with his big greasy fingers, and handed one to me and then one to her.

"Let's pass the whole plate next time, Dave," my mother said. "It's more polite that way."

Dave froze; his face suddenly drooped; his nose twitched and I was certain he would cry. "Table manners! I forget about table manners."

"It's all right, Dave."

"I used to have them, but they got lost!" Dave said, his eyes brimming.

"We'll get them back," my mother said. "Just eat for now."

And Dave obeyed. He was not wrong about his table manners. In fact, I had a hard time finishing my meal; I couldn't eat and watch him at the same time. Dave concluded his meal by smacking his lips loudly and sucking clean each finger. "Was there any pie?"

"Yes, Dave," my mother said evenly. "We'll have some pie—when everyone else is done."

Dave looked down, shamefaced.

After supper, I drove Dave back to jail, with my mother sitting in the middle.

Hawk Bend came into sight.

"I hate that damn jail," Dave said suddenly.

"You only have a few more days," my mother offered.

"People coughing and farting and snoring all night . . ."

I laughed. My mother gave me an annoyed look.

"You have to remember all that when you get out— how bad it is," she said to him. "That'll keep you on the straight and narrow." I braked at the tall brick building.

"The straight and narrow was always too narrow for me," Dave said.

We walked Dave inside. My mother signed off on a clipboard; the jailor initialed it. "Same thing tomorrow?" my mother said.

"You got him," the jailor said. "Our pleasure, believe me."

Dave pushed his mug at the jailor's face. "I had homemade fried chicken and apple pie for supper— what'd you have?"

"Let's go, Dave," the jailer said, and prodded him sharply forward.

As we left, I heard doors clang deeper in the jail, and then catcalls greeting Dave's return. In cheerful reply, Dave said, "I had homemade fried chicken and apple pie tonight. What'd you $@#$@$##&**% losers have?"

My mother flinched. "Goodness!"

We passed the Shell station where Tim was on night duty, then stopped at the Dairy Queen for three vanilla cones to go. Heading out of town, we approached the back of the Hawk Bend city limits sign. It was slightly tilted. I'd always felt some small sadness attached to that sign. It was stuck exactly between things—not city or country, not one place or another.

9

In my third week of work, the middle of June, longer days and hotter weather brought tourists in droves. They arrived in car after car, station wagon after station wagon, from Minneapolis and North Dakota and Iowa and Illinois and Indiana, all of them desperate to reach the lakes, cabins, and resorts.

I waited on creaking motor homes that sighed slowly into the station and docked at the far pumps, square tin schooners driven by middle-aged captains whose nightmares were of dead-end roads without sewage dumps.

I waited on station wagons jammed with kids and manned by dads in shorts, black socks, and Hush Puppies, fathers who called out, "Everybody try the bathroom—no souvenirs or candy—there's food in the cooler. Five minutes and we leave without you."

And, on the hottest days, I waited on the summer girls. In their fathers' long and boatlike Oldsmobiles, Buicks, and Cadillacs, the girls came to town for outboard-motor gas and ice cream. Fresh from waterskiing, wearing swimsuits that left the damp dark shapes of their bodies on the upholstery, they emerged in gleaming curves and smelled of coconut oil. They opened the trunk to clusters of orange fuel cans, which I removed and filled with a 50-to-1 gas and oil mixture. Barefoot, the girls shrieked at the hot pavement as they went to the freezer for Eskimo Pies, then returned to the pumps where I knelt, topping off their tanks. Ice cream dripped from their wrists and fingers onto the concrete, and sometimes onto their tanned and pink-tipped toes. The paler arches of their feet, as if dipped in a bowl of sugar, carried sand from the beach—a sparkling curve of granules that sprinkled their anklebones. As the girls ate ice cream, their smooth brown thighs shivered and sent goose bumps unfurling, like a gust of wind on smooth water.

"Gawd—I can't believe how much water went up my nose that last time!"

"Did you see DeeDee! She did a triple flip!"

"She didn't come up for a long time 'cause she lost her top."

They giggled wildly.

I worked there, crouched beside their fuel tanks, my face eye-level with the damp bottoms of their bathing suits, which smelled like sand and reeds and wet maple leaves, and I was glad my pants were baggy.

On Tuesday afternoon, I made a parts run uptown for Kirk, whose frequent "service calls" had left him with a backlog of real mechanical work. I passed by Elmo's Barbershop, which seemed empty and sad these days, and neared the NAPA Auto Store. Through the window I saw a man at the counter with a black bushel-basket of hair. I froze. It was the van man. The yellow Volkswagen peace-van man.

I considered retreating; he had not seen me.

Kirk needed the Ford thermostat, however, so I stepped inside. Along the counter—stacked with huge master catalogs of car parts—were the usual hangers-on, local men wearing caps and perched on stools, smoking cigarettes, in no hurry for their parts. On the wall, the Snap-on Tool and American Wheel Bearing and Midas Muffler calendar girls smiled down on everybody.

The store was weirdly silent except for a radio in back that played a Hank Williams song. Nobody was saying anything. They stared at the van man, who smiled pleasantly, arms folded, as he waited his turn.

"Who's next?" the manager, Dick Andrews, said evenly. A good auto-parts man was analytical, logical, open-minded. The best had the least personality, and Dick Andrews, with his wide-set, heavy-lidded eyes, was world-class.

"I've got a 1960 Volkswagen van, four cylinder, 1300 cc," the van man said to Dick. "I need a set of piston rings and sleeves." His hands were oil-stained and smudged.

Dick winced at the word Volkswagen but dutifully began to fan pages of an oversize parts book.

"Ain't in stock," one of the hangers-on said immediately.

The hippie held his half smile without looking about.

"Probably right," Dick said, not looking up and not slowing the fan of pages beneath his rubber-tipped thumb, "but let's check."

"That's because this is an American auto-parts store," one of the seed-cap fellows said. He winked at the other boys, who grunted with laughter.

Dick stopped on a particular page, ran his finger down it. "Sorry, don't carry those," he said to the van man, clapping shut his big book. "Fargo is your best bet."

"Well, I'm sort of stuck here," the hippie said. "Could you order them for me?"

"I could," Dick Andrews said noncommittally. He totted up the price, showed it to the van man.

"Ouch," the van man said.

"Cash up front, it'd have to be," Dick added, with the faintest note of apology in his voice. He looked past the van man to the street.

The van man was silent. He stroked his beard for some time. "If I ordered them, how long . . . ?"

"One week minimum. Truck comes on Thursdays."

"Well, I guess I'm not going anywhere," the van man said pleasantly. "I'll get back to you." As he turned he spotted me: me and my Shell station uniform. "Hello again, brother," he said. His dark eyes glowed briefly larger, then he passed by and out the door.

We all stared after him. Then the hangers-on started up.

"Cripes, did you smell him?"

"What a freak!"

"I hear they're camped out in the state forest west of town, a whole family of them."

"Paul? What can I do for you?" Dick said to me in his usual voice.

"The Ford thermostat Kirk called in?"

Dick nodded and disappeared into the back. I thought of the peace van, its curtains. A family?

"Living right in the damn bus. Crap in the woods like animals."

"Raccoons are cleaner than that. At least they know enough to wash in the river."

"I hear the woman was around asking for food or work."

"Ought to arrest them for vagrancy."

"Jail food, that would teach 'em a lesson or two."

"Little kids, too. You wonder what kind of life they have."

"Ought to take kids away from people like that."

"Here you go, Paul," Dick said evenly.

I signed for the thermostat and headed for the door. Behind me Dick said, "Who's next?"

That evening I told my father about the hippie van. We were by the machine shed, working on the mower, fitting it with new sickle sections in preparation for the second hay cutting. I was surprised to hear myself speak—but then we always talked better when there were tools passing back and forth between us.

As I related what Kirk had done to the hippies my

father slowly stopped cranking on his ratchet. He looked up at me from underneath the mower. There was a smudge of grease on his cheek. "Loosened the oil plug?"

I swallowed and nodded.

"On purpose?" he said, raising up on his elbows.

I nodded.

He laid down his wrench and sat up. Carefully, thoughtfully, he wiped his hands one finger at a time, then leaned back against the tire and chewed on a piece of grass for a spell. "You couldn't have stopped him?"

"It happened so fast," I replied. "Plus I wasn't sure he had really done it." I told him about seeing the van man in the auto-parts store.

He shook his head sadly, then bent again to his work. "God will punish Kirk. You can be sure of that."

I heard a noise over my shoulder. My mother, passing to the garden, had paused to listen. She had heard everything. "That doesn't help those poor people right now," she said.

As my parents and I drove through town, I glanced at the station and slouched an inch lower in the seat. I could have kicked myself for mentioning the subject of the hippie van. The last thing I needed was trouble at work. But we proceeded straight through the stoplight past the station, and headed west into the sun.

"You said the state forest. Any idea where these people are?" my father asked. He drove, and was not happy about it.

I shook my head.

Ten miles west of town we pulled into Milo's Bait Shop and Gas. In the cool interior, minnow tanks hissed and gurgled. Milo himself soon appeared from his trailer house, which was connected, and from which came the sound of *The Lawrence Welk Show* and the smell of bacon. Milo was a wizened man with fingers bent like fishhooks.

"Yup. I've seen 'em. They come walking in here once. Right through that door." He pointed.

"They're camped around here somewhere?"

Milo nodded. "Up there off the gravel road near Duck Lake. Just out of sight of the highway. Lot of traffic by there," he said. He leaned forward and whispered. "They say the woman most of the time don't wear a stitch of clothes."

"I doubt that," my mother said sharply.

"That's only what I hear," Milo said defensively. He glanced back toward the trailer, *The Lawrence Welk Show*, the even stronger smell of bacon. "Any minnows, leeches, or crawlers today?"

We found the yellow van. Its rear end was tilted up a foot and late sun blossomed in a green army-surplus parachute rigged as a porch roof.

To the side a small circle of blackened rocks ringed a tiny fire, atop which, dangling from a tripod of sticks, was a small kettle and the skinny, burnt legs of what could have been a rabbit or a squirrel. The van man rose to greet us. Two small children, as mosquito-bitten as if they had chicken pox, stood up to stare. A woman with very long hair, a tie-dyed shirt, and heavy breasts stepped from the van.

"Peace, friends," the van man said.

"Good day," my mother said.

The hippie mother smiled cautiously.

"Will you have a cup of tea and a bite to eat?" the van man said.

"We've had supper, thanks," my father said.

"We usually don't eat flesh," the mother said apologetically, turning toward the fire, "but we're low on rice."

The van man turned to me. "Hello yet again, brother."

I nodded.

"Paul tells me your van broke down," my father said.

The man nodded to my father. "A slight oil problem." He glanced at me again.

"Piston rings and sleeves are more than slight," my father said.

On the road a carload of locals drove by slowly, staring at the van. The bigger child stepped behind her mother.

"Relatively speaking—to the earth, to human happiness—piston rings are slight matters," the hippie said, "though another part of me hears and agrees with you."

"Where are you bound?" my father asked.

"San Francisco. Berkeley in particular. We're spreading teach-ins against the war."

"When do you have to be there?" my mother added.

"When we are supposed to," the van man said. "Arriving is less important than the journey."

My father glanced at my mother, then at the shabby campsite, at the children. Another vehicle, a pickup, passed slowly on the road; country music thumped from its radio, and its occupants, several boys, rubbernecked unashamedly. One of them shouted something.

"Do you have tools?" my father asked.

The van man nodded. "All but a taller jack. Though I think I've found a strong tree limb that I can use as a fulcrum, then some river stones to block up the rear end."

My father looked again at the smallest child, who was playing near the wheel.

"I have a hydraulic jack at home," my father said. "You could use it."

The van man smiled and bowed slightly. "Thank you. I accept."

"I'll bring it around tomorrow," my father said.

"Glen Allen," my mother said, "may I speak with you a second?" She pulled him over by our pickup.

The van man turned to me. "Your parents are proof that there is goodwill in the world."

"I guess," I shrugged.

He extended his hand. "Is."

"Is?"

He nodded. "That's my name."

"Paul Sutton." We shook hands; Is hooked my thumb with his and turned our palms in to each other.

"That's the peace handshake," he said. Behind me, my parents were speaking to each other; rather, my father was listening. My mother nodded again toward the children.

Is introduced the rest of his family. "This is Rising Moon." The tie-dyed mother smiled at me.

"And Safflower." He pointed to the larger child, a girl of about six, who frowned at me from behind her mother's skirts.

"And Soybean."

The toddler turned; she smiled, then came bumbling forward and clamped her arms around my leg.

"She feels your good heart," Rising Moon said.

"She likes your soul," Is agreed.

Luckily my parents returned. My mother smiled at the sight of the child attached to my leg. I didn't know what to do so I just stood there. "Glen Allen and I were wondering," she began, "if you might want to park your van on our farm."

"Just for a few days," my father added. "Until you get your van fixed and can be on your way."

The van with the hippie family towed easily behind the pickup. My father always carried a log chain for such occasions, and Is manned the yellow van's steering wheel as our little caravan rolled down the highway toward town. I sat on the outside, my parents together.

My father looked sideways at my mother.

"The children," she said. "I was worried about those

kids, especially the little one—if they're getting enough to eat."

"They might have thought of that before they started cross-country," my father said, glancing in his mirror.

My mother was silent. Then she said, "Maybe it's good to take chances in life."

My father didn't reply. Through the chain I could feel the bump and tug of the hippie van. I looked in the right side mirror. Behind us, following always at the same distance, the bright bus was like a new little planet attached to our own.

In town we slowed for the stoplight, which of course turned red. This left us on display dead center in Hawk Bend. Several locals slowed their pickups and turned to stare at our convoy. It was a long red light, but soon we were on our way again. Just about through town, passing the drive-in, my luck gave out. Kirk's blue Chevy was parked at the Dairy Queen with a highway view.

"There's Kirk," my father said.

"Maybe he won't see us," I said quickly. Then felt foolish.

My father glanced at me, then drove on.

Through the back window I saw Kirk suddenly pull out of the drive-in and accelerate behind us. He passed us, craning his neck at the peace van. Is gave Kirk the peace sign. Kirk glared and turned sharply, headed back to town.

"What will you tell him tomorrow?" my mother said, concern in her eyes.

"Paul will tell him the truth," my father said. "The truth sets us free."

And gets us beaten to a pulp. But I didn't speak.

At the farm it was sundown. We towed the peace van between the garden and the machine shed, parked it there close to vegetables and tools.

"And running water," my father said to Is and Rising Moon. "There's cold water from the hose and warm water in the milk house. Plus soap. Use as much soap and water as you like."

My mother nudged him.

"Many thanks, brother," Is said. Then he and Rising Moon looked about, did some kind of strange circle, pointing skyward in all four directions, and afterward turned to us and smiled. Butch, our old Labrador, raced up with tail wagging, and buried his nose in Rising Moon's crotch. She let him sniff.

"Butch!" my mother called.

"It's very peaceful here," Is said, nodding, looking about the farm.

"We like to think so," my father said, unhooking the chain.

"Tomorrow I'll show you around the farm," my mother said, shooing away Butch with a discreet but sharp boot to the flank. "You're welcome to all the milk you can drink, plus there's fresh eggs as well."

"Thank you so much," Rising Moon said, and hugged my mother.

"The hydraulic jack is just inside the shed," my father added. "Use what tools you need. We'll get you back on the road in no time."

"No time," Is repeated. "Interesting." As he launched forth on time in general and clocks in particular, for some reason I turned toward the van, to a rear window. There I saw another face, a girl with long pale hair framing an oval face and brown eyes. She was my age. As our eyes met she quickly drew the curtain.

10

At the station the next morning, Kirk arrived early. I could see him through the window as we drove up. After my mother handed me my lunch bag, I lingered briefly in the truck.

"Everything all right?" she asked.

"Sure," I said.

As I walked in, Kirk said, "Sutton, I saw something crazy last night."

Bud, in his usual stance—elbows on the glass counter, gumming Planter's peanuts—glanced at Kirk, then stared off toward the intersection again.

"Oh yeah?" I said as I stashed my lunch bag in its usual spot.

"Yeah. Real strange," Kirk said.

I found a clean grease rag, secured my tire gauge in my left breast pocket. "What would that be?" I asked.

"It would be you, Sutton. You and your old man towing that hippie van."

Bud turned to look at me. I fastened my till key on its little chain that ran from my belt to my pocket, did all my usual routines.

"That wasn't really you, Sutton," Kirk said. "Tell me I was dreaming."

"It was me." I stared at him briefly, then found a broom and began to tidy up the front office.

"Why would you be towing the hippie van?" Kirk said.

I swept up two cigarette butts and a scattering of Spanish peanut husks. Then I stopped and looked up. "Because you screwed him over."

Kirk stared at me. He grinned—and a moment later had me face against the wall locked in a hard half nelson. I didn't know anyone could move that fast: in an instant my free arm was yanked high behind my back, my forehead mashed into the fan belts on the wall. "You went and told your old man, right?"

I grunted. He was breaking my arm.

"And then you Good Samaritans went to help out the hippies, yes?"

I grunted in pain. "Yes . . ."

Bud coughed lightly. Politely.

"Well, this is the kind of help those creeps need, Sutton," he said, ratcheting my arm an inch higher, "help out of town—not back in."

Bud coughed louder.

Kirk loosened his grip. I flexed my arm and stumbled back. I still had my broom, and I brandished it at him. "Go to hell!" I blurted.

"Well, well, Sutton," Kirk said, laughing at the broom. "I thought your kind were supposed to turn the other cheek. And now you've started swearing, too." He squared his body to me, lowered his center of gravity as if coiling to strike.

"Morning, gentlemen!" Mr. Davies' voice called as he came through the back-room door.

"Morning, boss," we all said in unison. I managed to be sweeping the floor as he arrived.

Bud said later, "Your arm all right?" He touched my shoulder briefly.

"Yeah. Thanks," I said, though it ached badly. I felt worse about raising the broom in anger. What had I expected to do with it?

Later in the morning, on an auto-parts run, I checked with Dick to see if the Volkswagen piston rings had arrived.

"No," Dick said with mild surprise. "The order's written up and ready to go"—he paged briefly through a folder, put his rubber-tipped finger on it—"but it's cash up front so I haven't sent it in yet."

I paused. "What's the total?"

Dick ran his finger to the bottom of the page. "I'd need $219.78."

"Ouch is right," I murmured.

One of the hangers-on looked up. "Volkswagen? You're not talking about that hippie van?"

I was silent; Dick refiled the order.

"That weirdo with the hair?"

"Thank you, Paul," Dick said as I signed for the other auto parts and headed for the door.

"I heard they're camped out now at some farmer's place," one of the cap boys said.

"Hell, you'd have to watch 'em day and night," another said. "They'd steal you blind."

"Me, I'd be more worried about my heifers with that weirdo around."

Behind me they all laughed.

Except Dick Andrews. "Who's next?"

At about ten a.m., with a couple of cars lined up for servicing and Kirk gone on a service call, the long black Cadillac of Harry Blomenfeld flowed up to the pumps.

"Criminy—it's Kid Can!" Bud said. He hustled into the men's room and clicked the lock.

I swallowed and headed out to the pumps.

The driver, wearing sunglasses and a faded blue short-billed hat, sat staring straight ahead. His jaw was set. Harry Blomenfeld, from the rider's seat, gestured at him with both hands.

"So put a slug in my brainpan," the driver said. "Let's just get it over with."

"Well, *can* you crawl under the car anymore? Yes or no? Answer me, Angelo!"

The driver set his jaw harder.

"No," Harry Blomenfeld said. "You told me so yourself."

"So give me the cement boots and drop me in the damn lake. Let the fish eat out my eyeballs."

"This don't have nothing to do with your eyeballs or any other kind of balls. It's your legs that aren't worth a damn anymore," Harry Blomenfeld said.

I felt like I was at home and had happened into the kitchen when my parents were arguing. Without the swearing, that is. I cleared my throat.

The driver turned his sunglasses my way. "What's your problem?"

I got ready to dive for cover.

"It's all right, son," Mr. Blomenfeld said, leaning over, speaking close across his driver's mug. "We were just wondering if you might have time to change the oil today."

"Change the oil? Yes, sir."

"When would be a good time?"

"Ah . . . any time. Right now, sir."

"You see?" Harry said to Angelo.

"I don't want some damn kid working on my car."

"He's a good kid. And anyway, you can stand there and watch him."

"You're damn right I will."

I felt my Adam's apple moving like a yo-yo.

"Where to, son?" Harry Blomenfeld said cheerfully.

In the front office I leaned up against the men's room door. "Mr. Blomenfeld wants an oil change," I whispered to Bud.

"Criminy!" Bud murmured through the closed door. "Why us?"

"What do I do?"

"Change his damn oil!" Bud said.

"I'll need some help on the drive," I said, meaning the gas pumps.

· 94 ·

"To heck with the drive," Bud said.

In the back room I removed the blocks from Mr. Heltjen's Pontiac and backed it outside. Then I prayed briefly that I would not be murdered in the flower of my youth, after which I opened the door and waved Angelo forward.

The Cadillac eased softly onto the blocks. Angelo killed the engine. Outside the car he was a pasty-faced, squashed, dumpy man, thick-chested and short-legged. He moved as stiffly as if his feet were bound or frozen. I realized that Angelo was at least seventy; also that his black hair was dyed, like Mr. Kendrigan the clothier's.

"I got my own oil," Angelo said, opening the trunk. "My own filter. Everything."

"Yes, sir."

"All you got to do is service the car. You don't touch anything else, right?"

"Right, sir."

Mr. Blomenfeld sat inside the car, reading a newspaper, the *Chicago Tribune*. My hands shook as I placed the hoist arms under the frame. I went twice to all four corners of the car, making sure that nothing would scrape or bend. Then I was ready to raise the hoist. Mr. Blomenfeld remained inside the car, puffing on a cigar now, rustling his newspaper.

"Well, what's the matter?" Angelo said.

"I . . . I'm wondering if Mr. Blomenfeld will be getting out?"

"Why would he have to get out?"

I swallowed. Inside my baggy pants my knees knocked like castanets. "Well, sir, station rules—insurance rules, actually—say that we can't raise the hoist with anyone inside a car. In case there's an accident."

"Accident? You mean like the car falling off the hoist?!" Angelo said, putting his flat face directly under mine.

I swallowed.

"Sorry, no problem," Mr. Blomenfeld said, opening his door. Fresh cigar smoke wafted forward. "I'll go up front and read the paper."

"Thank you, sir," I said.

"Don't mind Angelo. He's a little particular about his car."

"Yes, sir. It's a fine car," I said.

"You're damn right it is, kid," Angelo said.

"And, son," Harry Blomenfeld said, "the men's room is up front, right?"

I worked underneath the Cadillac as carefully as a scientist. My trouble light illuminated the underbelly— muffler, drive shaft, transmission, brake lines—all of which looked shiny and new.

"I don't drive this car in the winter," Angelo said, "not with the damn salt they put on the highways around here."

"No rust at all, sir."

"They ought to shoot the guys that spread all that salt."

"Yes, sir." I carefully rolled the oil sump beneath the Cadillac.

"Salt is hell on cars, and it's tough on roads and the winter birds, too. Did you know that birds eat the salt along the roads?"

"I hadn't thought of that, sir."

"Nobody thinks about the winter birds," Angelo said. "The chickadees. The nuthatches. The English sparrows. The grosbeaks."

I wiped clean the oil drain plug.

"Seven-eighths-inch socket," Angelo said.

"Yes, sir."

"Counterclockwise," Angelo said.

"Yes, sir."

"Otherwise you strip the threads on the pan."

I nodded.

"Stripping the threads on the oil pan would not make me happy."

"I'll be careful, sir." Slowly I eased back on the handle of my ratchet wrench until the plug loosened and began to drip. I set aside the wrench and used my fingers. Warm cashew-brown oil (not Brazil-nut black like the Mercedes' oil) began to plop over my hand. I snatched free the oil plug just ahead of the shiny cascade.

Angelo nodded. "Nice work."

"The oil doesn't look dirty at all, sir," I said, holding up the shining plug.

Angelo took my wrist, held it closer to the hot light-bulb as he inspected the plug for grit or metal shavings.

"That's because I change it every fifteen hundred miles," Angelo said. "Have since we bought the car new."

"That's pretty impressive," I said.

"New-car manuals say change the oil every three to five thousand miles. That's a crime," he said, finally letting loose my wrist.

"You could be right."

"Ought to shoot the engineers who wrote that."

I brought around the grease gun and followed Angelo's stubby, crooked forefinger to each grease fitting. As I worked, cigar smoke was suddenly stronger. "Son, is there somebody in the can?" Harry Blomenfeld said. "Or is it locked?"

"Just knock loudly on the door, sir. If nobody comes out, I'll be there in a jiffy."

"You want me to?" Angelo began.

"I can handle it." Mr. Blomenfeld sighed.

As the oil drained, I heard heavy thudding on the door up front.

There was silence except for the *drip-drip* of the oil.

The pounding came again, louder this time. As I winced, I must have looked like I was grinning.

"What's so funny, kid?" Angelo said.

"Nothing, sir."

"A man's gotta go, a man's gotta go!"

"Yes, sir. I'd better see what the trouble is."

"You do that," Angelo said.

Up front Harry Blomenfeld stood glaring at the men's room door.

I tapped lightly on the door. "Bud? You in there?"

"What?" Bud whispered.

"Oh, that's right—are you finished cleaning the john, Bud?"

There was silence.

"Mr. Blomenfeld needs to use it."

There was a brief flurry of whisking and scrubbing sounds, then the noise of a toilet flushing—after which Bud, white-faced and trembling, opened the door and rushed past us.

"About time," Harry Blomenfeld said sternly, and closed the door behind him.

Bud, seeking escape through the back room, hurried squarely into the barrel chest of Angelo. Bud bounced backward and froze; Angelo's hand went to his coat. The two men stared at each other. Bud's wide eyes flickered from Angelo's driver's cap down to his Italian shoes and back up; Angelo's squinty eyes took in Bud's tidy Shell uniform, his jaunty cap. His hand relaxed; he smiled at Bud. "Hi there," he said.

Bud blushed crimson.

Later, as I finished the Blomenfeld Cadillac, Bud worked the drive, pumping gas, washing windows, moving with an odd lightness to his step. It was the first time I'd ever seen him wash windshields. Angelo lingered in the doorway, his back to me, where he could see the pumps. Once I dropped a wrench and he whirled around at the clattering sound. "Geez, kid, don't scare me like that!"

"Sorry, sir."

He nodded and turned back to the driveway.

"All clear!" I said. The hoist sighed a long exhalation and slowly let down the Cadillac, its great tires touching concrete, swelling as they took on weight. The metal arms clanked weakly against the floor and were still. I let out a breath of my own, then wheeled around the vacuum. "Hey—where do you think you're going, kid?"

"I usually vacuum and do windows inside and out, sir. Our motto is 'extra service.'"

Mr. Blomenfeld leaned in the doorway, still scanning his paper. "Angelo can do that at home," he said.

Angelo tipped back his cap and shrugged. "I could," he said. "But what the hell's the hurry? Let the kid do it if he wants. He's a good kid. I like him."

Harry Blomenfeld lowered his paper and laughed; the bouquet of his cigar smoke filled the back room.

At that moment, Kirk, who had returned from his service call, walked into the station. He froze at the sight of the big Cadillac in the back room—and at Harry Blomenfeld and Angelo.

"This is a good kid you've got here," Angelo said, jerking his head at me. "Maybe the best one you've ever had—and you've had some real losers."

"Thanks," Kirk said. "Paul's new but we like him, too."

"I like him so much he's gonna be changing my oil from now on," Angelo said. "But only him."

"Sure, you bet," Kirk said.

"Good—then that's all set," said Angelo, clapping Kirk hard on the shoulder.

After work that day, my mother asked me about Kirk; if there was any trouble.

"Some," I said. My shoulder still ached.

"Anything we can help you with?"

"No, thanks," I said cheerfully. "Got it covered."

In the morning farmyard the yellow peace van, like a giant pumpkin in the garden, sat dew-covered and silent. Alongside the van, suspended in a hammock, was the dark outline of Is. He looked like a string-bean pod. On my way to work, I let the truck coast down the drive-way so as not to awaken the guests.

"Are the Volkswagen parts here yet?" my mother asked.

"No." I told her about the matter of cash up front.

She was silent. "Rising Moon and I have had some good talks. She's really very nice."

At the Shell station the traffic was heavier now as June tipped toward July. There was a quickened flow of station wagons jammed with coolers, tents, sleeping bags, plus boat trailers filled with inner tubes and water skis and outboard motors. Windshields were crazy entomol-ogy experiments. Iridescent insect heads and the brit-tle gauze of dragonfly wings, trapped in the angles of windshield-wiper arms, crackled and broke as I swept them away. Fragments of monarch butterflies and hulking yellow bumblebees—some still alive and flexing—clung to bumpers and grilles. Wasps were hardiest; half of one stung me through my damp leather windshield chamois.

At noon that day, when, magically, the tourists had all stopped somewhere else for ice cream and toilets, when everyone in Hawk Bend sat eating a plate of hot beef and gravy, when I alone watched the intersection, the shiny Leikvold station wagon pulled in.

Peggy. She wore a polka-dot bathing-suit top and short-shorts. "Hi, Paul."

Paul. My own name from the lips of Peggy Leikvold.

"Dale," she continued. "Have you seen him lately?"

My shoulders sagged slightly. "I guess so, yes," I said, pretending to think back.

"When?" she said quickly.

"A few days ago."

"A few days ago when?"

"On Thursday."

"Darn," she breathed. She looked through the windshield.

In the back of the station wagon were pom-poms, and orange-and-black wool marching-band outfits as well as the tall silver hat and skinny baton of her father, the bandleader.

"We were gone all week for these stupid parades," she said, "in these stupid towns with their stupid summer festivals and their stupid floats." She was assistant bandleader, helping out her father one last summer. Her brown cleavage swelled with each "stupid."

"Sorry," I said.

She didn't hear me. "Well, what did he say?"

I paused. "He said, 'Tell her I asked if she asked about me.' "

She stared. "That's all?"

I nodded.

She pinched the tip of her tongue between her teeth as she thought about that. I watched as her blue eyes glazed over. A flush began in her cheeks, dropping like a slow, crimson movie curtain down her neck, then spreading its fine red tassels down her chest.

"Listen, Paul," she said suddenly. "Do me a favor?"

"Sure."

"Call him for me?"

"Call him? I guess. Okay."

She nodded. Her shiny eyes were locked on mine.

"What do I say?"

"Tell him . . . tell him . . . I asked if he asked if I asked about him."

I smiled. "Okay. When?"

She looked through me, to somewhere I couldn't see. "Call him right now."

Inside the office I dialed the number of Bender's Sawmill. I did not have to look it up—she knew it. Just the two of us at the telephone, Peggy leaning close to the receiver, and me taking in all her midsummer bouquet of scents: hair spray, antiperspirant, chewing gum on her faintly coppery breath.

The phone rang twelve times. I turned to her.

"No, wait," she whispered urgently.

"Yeah?" someone said on the twentieth ring. In the background I could hear the wail of a saw.

"Is Dale there?"

"Yeah. Who needs him?"

"This is . . . the Shell station in town. He's got a . . . fan belt here."

"Hang on."

I handed the receiver to Peggy. Her eyes widened and she pushed it back to me.

"Yeah?" Dale said in the same voice as the other speaker.

"This is Paul," I said, speaking loudly, "at the Shell station?"

In the background the saw's whine dampened; something clattered as the door closed.

"Sutton," Dale's voice said, closer now. "So what's new?" In the black curve of the receiver I saw his grin, his dark waterfall of hair.

"Peggy came in. She has a message for you." Beside me Peggy leaned closer, a firm, oblivious breast on my bare arm.

"So what was it?" Dale said.

"She said to tell you that she asked if you asked if she asked about you."

There was silence. Then I heard him laugh. "She said that?"

"Word for word."

"What was she wearing?"

"Wearing?" I looked at Peggy. She leaned back self-consciously.

"A polka-dot bathing-suit top and white short-shorts."

"Did she look good, Sutton?"

I looked straight at Peggy. "She looked great. Tops, believe me."

Peggy covered her mouth and laughed. Her eyes dropped, for a moment, to the name tag sewn on my shirt.

"A bathing-suit top and short-shorts," Dale said. "Damn."

Outside, the driveway bells ding-dinged. "Listen, I gotta go."

"Sutton—wait," Dale said. "Tell her I want to see her."

"Okay. When?"

"Soon. Today."

"Today. Where?"

There was silence. "It's got to be on the sly," Dale said. "Her old man, this damn town—you know how it is."

Outside another car pulled up.

"Meet her here at the station," I said. It just popped out, but it only made sense—plus somebody had to take charge.

"You nuts, Sutton?"

"If you go uptown, somebody sees you. You drive outside of town, someone sees you for sure."

"Yeah, it's always that way. I'm listening, Sutton."

"Here at the station you're a customer, she's a customer. If there's no one around, you can talk in the back room."

There was silence. "I owe you one, Sutton."

"Four o'clock this afternoon!" Peggy blurted into the phone.

"Hey!" Dale said. "Hey!"

She hung up the phone and hurried off, leaving me to a driveway of impatient tourists.

At a quarter to four I heard Dale's car come through the intersection. He drove a 1955 Chevy stripped and primed in flat gray. Its stock 283-cubic-inch block had been jerked, the engine compartment torched wider, and the motor mounts strengthened for the 409 block—which itself had been bored, stroked, and blueprinted in a Minneapolis machine shop. The transmission was a Hurst four-speed, the drive train beefed up, the suspension stiffened, the rear-end differential geared at 4:68 for maximum quarter-mile time—said to be in the low thirteen-second range. It was the engine's camshaft, however, direct from a speed shop somewhere in California, that gave the car its signature note: a rough, throaty idle that the mechanically uninformed mistook for an engine in need of tuning.

I looked up from the tire machine as Dale's Chevy trembled by. Only its thickened rear tires—six-inch slicks—gave it away. No stupid flames or racing stripes painted down the sides, no leaf-spring risers for a jacked-up rear end, no bright hubcaps. Dale, casing the station, nodded once at me. A jerk of his sharp chin. There was no sign of Peggy, and he was early, so I made a brief, circling motion with an upraised index finger. He nodded again ever so slightly, and headed uptown to make a loop down Main Street.

At precisely four o'clock Dale rumbled up to the back-bay doors and killed his engine. I went over. He was freshly scrubbed, wore a clean white T-shirt, and smelled strongly of English Leather cologne.

"You seen her?" he said. His voice was stiff and throaty.

"Not yet."

He looked around nervously, then popped his hood and pretended to check his oil—which allowed me a good look at the engine: its gleaming chrome valve covers; the two four-barrel carburetors that jutted upward like raised aluminum fists. "She was there, Sutton, on the damn phone when you were talking," Dale said accusingly.

"She didn't want to talk to you. What was I supposed to do? Give me a damn break!" I said. Dale turned and raised one dark eyebrow at me. My eyes widened slightly.

"I guess," he muttered. His stare went to the back room, where Kirk's legs, on a creeper, protruded from beneath a Pontiac. A scattering of muffler clamps and bright pipe lay alongside, and his air hammer rattled. The second bay, the car wash, was occupied. And the driveway was rapidly filling with tourists. "I thought you said we could talk here. How the hell we gonna do that?"

"The busier the better." I shrugged.

He narrowed his eyes to consider that.

At that point Mr. Davies came out carrying his bank deposit bag and the mail.

"New tires?" I said loudly. "Certainly, Dale. Let's take a quick look in the warehouse."

Mr. Davies nodded. "Keep up the good work, Sutton."

Tucked behind the station was a small log building, one of the town's original structures, I suppose, and now used as a warehouse for tires and cases of oil. Its thick walls made it thief-proof. Dale Bender followed me through the low door. I pulled the lightbulb chain. The building was close with the smell of fresh black butyl. Long tunnels of tires, stacks of tires in the corners, tires rising to the ceiling, thirteen-inch boat-trailer tires to fifteen-inch Oldsmobile rims, even hard-rubber sixteen-inch tires for Model-T Ford rims, now used mainly on homemade trailers. I turned to Dale and gestured at the shadowy spaces of the warehouse. "You can talk back here."

"You nuts, Sutton? She ain't gonna come back here."

"Well, the car wash, then," I said, annoyed.

Dale looked at me.

"Take it or leave it," I heard myself say. "I got customers." Astoundingly, Dale did not deck me.

"Maybe she ain't coming," Dale muttered.

"She'll come," I said.

When we returned, the Leikvold station wagon sat at the far pumps, facing away as if for a quick exit.

"Geez, Sutton, you're right—there she is," Dale breathed. "What do I do?"

"Pretend to work on your car."

He turned to his engine.

I hurried across the drive, starting gas on two other cars, then went to Peggy.

"He's here!" she said even as I approached; there was fear in her eyes. She looked through her rearview mirror at Dale's Chevy. "What do I do?"

As I looked back, a car emerged, dripping and shiny, from the wash bay. I looked down at the tidy, dust-free Ford Safari wagon. "Car wash today, miss?" I said, and saluted.

She looked back into the wash bay with its tall open door. Water dribbled from little nozzles and the big mechanical mops hung trembling and wet. She grinned at me. "Yes," she murmured. "Definitely."

As I worked the pumps I watched her pull up to the wash-bay door. Dale's Chevy stood just a few feet away. He pretended to fiddle with his engine, but I guessed they were talking. Then Dale glanced around and slipped inside the Ford wagon. Peggy accelerated sharply into the bay. The door rattled down over the rising hiss of water; then, starting slowly but gathering speed, the spinning brushes began their *slappa-slappa-slappa.*

12

Tim owed me an hour, so I left early that afternoon. Dale and Peggy were gone by then, Dale's Chevy
easing out of town north, Peggy speeding home in the
cleanest station wagon in Hawk Bend. Four washes,
four spin cycles, four rinses, and afterward the Leikvold
wagon soared from the humid wash bay wet and gleaming.

I needed to clear my head of Dale and Peggy, so I
walked uptown to the library. A regular visitor, particularly in the summers, I had not been to the library since I
began work at the station. I hardly read anything anymore—certainly not my Bible.

The Hawk Bend library had white columns with
swallows' nests mudded underneath the cornices, and
tall honeysuckles growing up beside a flight of sharp-
edged granite steps. I liked how it looked and felt inside: the deep silence; the even rows of books on their
tall shelves; the rolling ladder with a greased track above
and little wheels below; the long, heavy reading tables
with sturdy oak chairs; the arched windows showing
dusky daylight. I could see why people went to real
churches.

"Hello there, Sutton," said Miss Verhoven. She was the tall, square-shouldered head librarian, an unmarried woman in her late fifties. Her reddish-gray hair was cut like a helmet, and her imposing desk faced the main doors. From this central position she monitored all parts of the library, ensuring that readers did not stray from their sections. Books were arranged in the Hilda Verhoven alphanumeric system: "W.21+" meant books for women twenty-one and older; "M.21+" meant books for men twenty-one and older; "B.13+" meant books for boys over thirteen; "G.13+" meant books for girls over thirteen—and so on.

"You're looking well today, ma'am."

"Two books maximum, Sutton," Miss Verhoven said. "You know the rules." Her two-book rule was iron-clad.

"Yes, ma'am," I said, and flashed her a smile. "You're always ahead of me." I tried to butter her up whenever I could. I figured she liked the attention and this was why she let me read a couple years beyond my real age—though it was possible she felt sorry for me: there was a misconception in town that kids in the Faith were denied all books but the Bible.

"No, Sutton, I just have a good memory." She rapidly riffled through a recipe box of 3 × 5 cards. "You still have two at home."

"You're absolutely right, ma'am," I said.

"Newspapers or magazines today, then, Master Sutton," she said.

"I'm looking for something in particular," I said. "Gangsters in the 1920s in St. Paul?"

"Gangsters." As she thought about that, her eyes squinted and crossed slightly. "The *Minneapolis Tribune* is your best bet."

"Yes, ma'am."

"I keep my newspapers in the basement storeroom," she said.

"Yes, ma'am." I'd never been permitted there. The basement, yes, which was where kids' books were housed, but never the storeroom.

"If I let you down there, you wouldn't get them in the wrong piles?"

"No, ma'am."

"All right then, Sutton," she said. She rattled her drawer, removed a large iron key on a brass ring, and reluctantly handed it over.

In the basement room, dim light shone down from the filmy windows grown over with ferns, or at least their image: past rains had overflowed gutters and splashed straight onto ferns, slapping their muddy fronds against the glass, leaving dried, fossil-like patterns behind. As my eyes adjusted, before me in the gloom were the newspapers—bales of them standing in rows, like Stonehenge. Each stack was tied neatly at the top with a butterfly knot of twine. At floor level were rusty tins, set at even intervals, of mothballs, rat poison, and nitrogen fertilizer. The fertilizer drew moisture from the air and kept the papers from molding.

I chose a bundle from 1925 and began scanning headline articles. The dust made me sneeze, and I glanced guiltily toward the stairs. But only a little way into the pile—beginner's luck—I saw the name "Kid Can Blomenfeld." The article was about bootlegging. It included other names such as Alvin "Creepy" Karpis, George "Machine Gun" Kelly, "Dapper" Danny Hogan, Homer Van Meter. An editorial objected to corrupt Twin Cities police; how out-of-town criminals from Chicago and New York were welcome to hide out in St. Paul. The writer called it the "St. Paul Layover," and its rules, he wrote, were simple:

> Check in on arrival, pay off the officials, and commit no crimes within the city limits. A gangster's Mecca, some of whom are reputed to have bought lake homes in northern Wisconsin and Minnesota to be closer to the Canadian border. Life in the north allows gangsters to escape the heat—in more ways than one!

I let out a breath. There were more articles, but I would be late to meet my mother at the station. I marked the bundle, carefully retied the twine, and hurried upstairs to daylight.

"Find what you're looking for, Sutton?" Miss Verhoven called.

"Mostly," I said. "Though I'm wondering if you have any *Chicago Tribune*s."

She gave me a long look. "Gangsters, the *Chicago Tri-bune*—you must be curious about Mr. Blomenfeld."

My eyes widened.

She pursed her narrow lips. "It was just a guess. He's one of our more famous—some would say infamous—citizens. He comes here to the library with regularity."

"The gas station, too," I said.

"*And*, Sutton?" she said.

I swallowed. Lowered my voice. "I was just wondering, you know, if what they say about him is true?"

"What do they say about him, Sutton?"

I lowered my voice still further. "That he was a gangster. That he once—"

"I believe that is all true," she said evenly.

"It is?"

"Yes. But I ask you, Sutton, how has he treated you at the station?"

"Well, fine," I said.

"Me, too," she said. "I've always found Mr. Blomenfeld to be a gentleman. He reads a lot, and takes very good care of the books he borrows. He's become a regular patron here, and I have every reason to believe that his past is behind him."

I was silent.

"Now, I can order those *Chicago Tribune*s," Miss Verhoven said. "If you still want them."

I thought about it for a moment or two. "I guess not."

For the first time ever, she actually smiled at me.

"Then be on your way, Master Sutton. We've both got work to do."

Coming home after work, I saw a small plume of smoke rising by the garden, by the yellow peace van, whose parachute silk glowed in sunlight. There was a perfect ring of fieldstone around a campfire. "They prefer to cook outdoors," my mother said.

I drove past the garden. Is sat cross-legged, with back straight, and looked thoughtfully into the distance.

"I thought he was going to pull his engine today," I said.

"He said he first needed to get his 'psychic-terrestrial bearings,'" my mother said. At the sound of the pickup, Is looked up and gave us the peace sign.

Then Rising Moon stood up from among the thick tomato plants—and kept rising, and not one moon but two appeared: her great, bare breasts gleamed in the sunlight. She waved.

My mother made a brief croaking noise, then clamped a hand hard over my eyes. Blinded, and knowing the cattle fence and feed bunker were to my right, I steered left and sideswiped the caragana hedge. I batted away my mother's hand and managed to steer the truck back onto the straight and narrow, and into the garage. Green stems clung to the driver's side mirror. My mother stared at me—then began to laugh.

I could not have been more annoyed.

And she could not stop laughing.

"It's not that funny," I said.

After supper I went to the barn for my evening chores. Inside I saw her—Is's older girl—at the calves' pen, her lank long pale hair hanging down as she petted a black calf.

"Hi there," I said.

She turned quickly. There was silence but for the thud and bump of the calves, who were hungry.

"Hi."

"My name is Paul," I said.

"Sorry about my mother," she blurted. "She's so embarrassing." With that she hurried past me, leaving a contrail scent of fresh bath soap and shampoo, the same kind my mother used. I went to the door and watched her walk quickly across the yard to the van, where she went inside and pulled the curtains.

In the house, I said to my mother in an offhand, passing way, "The Is family has an older girl."

"I know," my mother said. "Janet. She's sixteen."

I looked at my mother. "Why didn't you tell me?"

She paused a moment. "I think it has something to do with a mother's instincts."

I let out an annoyed sound, and stomped back outside. It was nine o'clock now, the sun lower but still tawny yellow. My father was walking over to the peace van, so I joined him.

"Hello, friends," Is greeted us, looking up from the campfire.

My father nodded.

"Some tea?" A copper pot hung from a tripod over the fire.

"No, thanks," my father said.

"Sit," Rising Moon said. She was dressed—mostly—in a long shift that had once been a man's shirt. Her breasts moved freely as she bent to swirl the teapot.

My father looked about for something to sit on, then settled onto the ground. I followed suit.

"Tea, Paul?" Rising Moon said, offering me a handleless cup.

"Sure," I said. The tea smelled like alfalfa and raspberries. As I held the rough pottery cup in my hand, my thumb kept reaching for a loop that did not exist. My eyes were on the van, its closed curtains.

"To the solstice!" Is said, holding up his cup to the summer sky. "Actually it's three days until summer solstice, but the light here is most friendly."

"Yes and no," my father said. "The long days mean more work for farmers."

"True," Is replied, leaning back. Then he launched forth on the necessity to maintain harmony with the seasons and "mind time" rather than submit to the tyranny of "mechanical time," which did not care about people but only the profits of industrial capitalism. My father glanced at me. From the rear of the van I heard rock music come on, and then the sudden crying of a baby. Rising Moon swore sharply, unpeaceably, and went into the van. There was a brief muffled argument, then the music stopped.

"Speaking of things mechanical," my father said to Is, "do you know the truth of what happened to your Volkswagen engine?"

Rising Moon, carrying the baby, Soybean, rejoined us at the fire.

"I have an idea," Is said, with no change of tone. He stared, eyes closed, full into the setting sun.

"Paul can tell you," my father said. "He saw it all."

"No matter now. Recourse is long-term and karmic," Is said.

"What goes around comes around!" Rising Moon added; she did not appear so forgiving.

"Thou shalt not hate thy brother in thine heart," Is said to her.

"Thou shalt not defraud thy neighbor, neither rob him," Rising Moon shot back.

"Leviticus," my father said.

"Very good," Is said.

"Chapter 19, I believe," my father added.

"Verse 16 or so," Is added, still without opening his eyes.

"You know the Scriptures," my father said. There was a new, lighter tone to his voice.

"All too well, I'm afraid," Is replied.

My father did not respond.

The baby continued to fuss, and Rising Moon

hoisted her shirt. My father coughed briefly and politely shifted his stance away, toward Is. I didn't. I watched the baby gurgle and suck, and I watched beyond, in the little porthole windows, for some sight of Janet. But she didn't appear.

"How did you get the name Is," my father asked.

"My given name was Israel Bronfman, but I changed it, legally, to Is."

"Just Is?"

Is nodded.

"Why?"

"From a loss of faith and a secular epiphany," Is said. "I came to believe that for the world to survive one of two things must happen. Either people must transform themselves or God must transform himself. And since God does not much manifest himself these days, then that is His sign—His implicit message—that we must change ourselves."

"I don't know that I'd agree with that," my father said evenly. "I think God is manifest in many ways. The growth of seeds. A new calf. A good day of work and fellowship."

"It's a sentimental view of God, but all right," Is allowed. "My main point is that people, not God, must save the world."

My father narrowed his eyes.

"The irony, of course," Is added, "is that to transform ourselves we must give up God and live strictly within the present—which for me, of course, is the 'is.' "

Above us in the weakening light, some nighthawks dipped and chattered.

"This—how you live—is saving the world?" my father said, gesturing to the battered van, the shabby family.

"It's a start," Is said.

Rising Moon finished nursing and held the sleeping Soybean up to her shoulder.

"What about your name, Rising Moon?" my father asked.

"Throughout history, women have mainly been reflected in the light of men, but nowadays we are rising." She looked pointedly at him.

My father stood up. "If you need help with the van, let me know. We don't want to keep you from your journey."

13

Saturday morning was fair and clear. Rising Moon and my mother worked and talked in the garden. Is read a book in his hammock. A wisp of smoke rose from the campfire. From the van I could feel Janet's eyes on me as I passed toward the machine shed.

On this fine June day, with the hay fields between first and second cutting, it was corn cultivating time. After a midweek rain, the corn was growing quickly, beginning to rustle at night as it neared knee height. There was time for one more pass through the field with the tractor and cultivator. Then, with the weeds smothered and the stalks banked up with a dust mulch, the corn "laid by," was on its own. In July the rains tapered off. With luck the corn would have stored enough moisture to get it through the dry weeks of August.

My father liked to say it was a metaphor of faith. Which I had little of these days. At night when I tried to read the Bible, I fell asleep within minutes. If I couldn't read or sleep, I listened to WLS out of Chicago and, even later at night, to rock-'n'-roll stations that came all the way from Little Rock and Memphis.

In the cool shed, I lay in the dirt attaching sharp new shovels on the tines of the cultivator. Then I saw her—

Janet—pass by the open door on her way to the barn. I glanced around, stood up, brushed myself off, and followed her. Inside the dusky barn, I found her petting the calves.

"Hi again," I said.

"Hi," she murmured.

"That one's only a week old," I said, pointing. She smiled shyly and rubbed his head.

"My name is Paul."

"I know," she said. "You said so last time we met."

I shrugged.

"Mine is Janet."

"I know."

She nodded. Her eyes caught my smile. "What's so funny?" she said.

"Nothing really. I was just thinking that we both have names that are"—I fumbled, felt my ears warm— "old-sounding."

She shrugged.

I bumbled something more, then said, "Well, I'd better get to work."

She turned back to pet the calves.

In the machine shed I climbed aboard the John Deere with its front-mounted cultivator, started the engine, backed out, and headed toward the field. Its shiny shovels and shields swayed as I drove. I looked back several times toward the barn and yard, but didn't see Janet.

At the field I forced myself to focus. I stopped and counted rows. It was crucial to begin cultivating on a matched set of four rows. Since we had used a four-row planter to seed the corn, the cultivator tines were spaced to match the planter rows. Many a farm kid had had his hide whipped, many a hired man had been sent down the road for getting "off row" and rooting out the young plants.

I kept thinking of Janet. Her shining long hair that hung down straight and thin as the rest of her. She was my age and had only pointy bumps for breasts; then again I was no Joe Weider.

I found my four rows and concentrated on the first round. The corn rows passed evenly between the tines, through the shields, and popped up straightly behind. The narrow shovels "scoured" as they should, and the loamy soil rolled up damp and warm against the stalks and corn roots. Mosquitoes, disturbed, filtered up from the fronds, and though the heat and noise of the engine dispersed most of them, a few drafted my back and found their way onto my neck and shoulders. I turned up my collar and drove on.

At field's end I levered up the cultivator, swung around for the next set of rows—and saw a flash of yellow in the woodlot along the field. I looked again but saw nothing. On the next round I kept a watch on the trees along the fence. I thought I saw her alongside a red oak— but it was only some leaves turned yellow. On the fourth round I saw Janet's hair, then an arm and a leg. She was leaning against a tree watching. I pretended not to see her. With each successive round I came closer.

Finally I looked up—pretended to suddenly see her—and waved. She smiled, and covered her ears against the tractor's noise. I headed downfield, occasionally looking over my shoulder. She came all the way to the fence now, and put her arms and chin on the post. She was still there when I returned. I kept looking back at her as I circled the field. Each time I passed, I waved and she waved. Once when I came around she had made a string of black-eyed Susans along the top wire. I pointed to it and held up my thumb. She smiled.

On the next round I braked to a halt. Letting the engine idle, I walked over to the fence. A post and four barbed wires separated us. "Great flowers."

"Thanks."

Then we were shy and silent.

"What are you doing to the field?" she asked.

"Cultivating weeds from between the corn rows. I just go round and round."

She toyed with the black-eyed Susans.

"Would you like a ride?"

She slipped quickly between the wires.

At the tractor I helped her aboard. "Be sort of careful," I said. She put a bare foot in my hand and I hoisted her up. Her legs were long and smooth as chamois. Her foot rose from my palm in slow motion, and her shirt rode up, revealing, for an instant, her flat white belly and the paler curving undersides of her breasts.

When she was aboard we started downfield. The tractor lurched slightly, which brought a small squeak from her, and we were under way. She stood rigid beside me on the iron platform, clutching the seat with one hand, her forearm stiff across my back, the other bare arm stretched out, frozen, to the headlight arm. As she rode along, her clean smell engulfed me and I could not keep my eyes from her bare arm, her hand. "Left!" she called to me.

"Sorry!" I corrected, saving a few corn plants but rooting out several others. "I'm not used to having company," I said.

"I can get off," she said quickly.

"No, no. I like the company," I said.

"Are you sure?"

"Positive." As I drove along I explained to her about the row spacing, about matched sets, about tractor hydraulics—the suave, sophisticated adventures of a corn cultivator like me. She actually seemed interested.

Back near the fence I slowed. "Well, here we are."

She looked ahead, her lips moving as she counted rows. "Are those the next four?" she said, and pointed down.

"Yes." I swung the steering wheel—one of my smoothest turns of the day—hoisting the cultivator with the hydraulic lever, arcing squarely into the next quad, dropping the tines dead on dirt, and we headed back up-field.

Gradually, after several more rounds, she began to sway with the undulations of the dirt below. I felt her spine loosen, her torso, her arms, her legs accept the rhythm of the machine. She did not mind, now, leaning against me.

"Want to try steering?" I called out.

"Sure."

I slowed, gave her the seat, and crouched beside her, my arm alongside hers.

"That's good!" I said. She drove straighter than I did. We laughed.

At field's end I had, of course, to make the turns, but she wanted to steer again, so this time I sat far back on the iron seat and gave her the front part. She sat between my thighs and steered, and I raised and lowered the cultivator when I had to and in this way we kept moving up and down the field. I do not remember much about the rest of that morning other than the warmth of her back against my chest, and her outstretched arms slowly flushing pink from sunlight, and the warm wash of June drifting through her hair and over me.

That evening, at supper, I was silent. The potatoes and meat came by on their platters. I took only small portions.

"Paul? Are you well?" my mother said.

"Yes. Just tired, I guess."

"Did you get the whole field done?" my father asked. He had been busy in the machine shed.

I nodded.

"It went well, I take it?"

"Sure. No problem."

Later in the evening my father drove back up the lane and into the yard. He walked briskly to the porch where I sat staring across to the peace van where Janet was cloistered.

"Paul, come with me please."

I nodded absently and got into the pickup. My father drove down the lane and back to the cornfield. The sun was lower now, which deepened the shadows and highlighted the corrugation of the rows—which no longer looked so parallel. The rows had gone from straight and narrow to wavering, almost paisley in the worst spots.

I stared.

"If I didn't know better, I'd swear you were drunk when you did this," he said. That vein throbbed in his forehead.

I looked over my shoulder to the yard. Janet's hair flashed as she swung one of the little kids around and around, and their laughing voices came faintly across the field. My father's eyes followed mine.

"I get it," he said. Then he reached into the rear of the truck. "Here's a hoe. I want you to repair every corn plant you tore out. Don't come back until it's dark. Do you understand?"

To spite him I worked until well after dark, when I could no longer see my way, and then the moon came up and I could see again. I kept working until the truck's headlights came down the lane and shone into the field. It was my mother come to take me home. "Paul," she called out. "Come in. It's time!"

"No, thanks. I'm fine," I said. And I was. I felt full of power, full of moonlight—I could have worked all night.

"Please, Paul," she said, "come home." Her voice broke.

I stood up, and only then felt the blisters on my hands, the deadness in my legs, the cold wetness of my dew-soaked jeans. For her, I shouldered my hoe and came in.

14

As I began another week of work at the station, my legs no longer ached from the concrete. My arms were tanned coppery from sunlight off pavement. The veins in them felt more pronounced and my shirt was tighter: fitting tires, lifting heavy rims, torquing down lug nuts, hammering away rusted muffler clamps—all of it had given me the beginning of muscles. I had also developed, from the continual glare off the yellow metal face of the station, a squint that I fancied was not unlike Elvis's. My hair was thicker and fuller. Yellow curls fell down my forehead and on the back of my shirt collar.

"Would Paul like a hair trim soon?" my father asked. My mother usually cut my hair, though a couple of times a year, as a gesture to the local economy, she took me to Elmo's Barbershop on Main Street.

"I can get one in town," I said casually.

"See that you do," my father replied. "Soon."

On this Monday, not long after I arrived at work, Peggy drove in. Her father's station wagon still gleamed. "Have you seen Dale?"

"I don't work weekends," I said, leaning toward her window, getting an excellent look down her blouse. Then

I squatted beside her door, eye level; I had not yet lost all principles.

"Damn. The marching band was gone again," she said. "I should quit. Why do I still help with the damn band? I've already graduated."

"Because of your father," I said.

"Because he pays me," she said. "Otherwise I'd have to be a carhop or do some other embarrassing job."

I sometimes forgot that the Leikvolds were not rich. Their handsome good looks—mother and father and daughter alike—were their main capital. "Good assistant bandleaders are hard to find," I said.

She smiled a little, glanced up at me, then toward the intersection. She bit her lower lip.

"If I see Dale, is there a message?"

"I don't know," she said. She toyed with her keys. "He kind of scares me."

I was silent.

"What are you thinking?" she asked.

"He scares me, too."

She laughed briefly. Then her face turned serious as she looked back to the intersection, to the stoplight. "I shouldn't be doing this. Fooling around when Stephen's gone."

I shrugged.

"It feels like all the other goings-on in this town."

My gaze slipped sideways to Kirk's blue Chevy.

"Everybody knows about *him*," she said.

"But you and Stephen are not married," I replied, "so it's not the same."

She turned back to me. "True."

I was silent.

"Objectively I know what it is," she said. "It's summer, it's hot, I'm in this phase right now." She looked down at herself—looked down at her body. "Sometimes it's like I itch all over," she said, staring at me.

I swallowed.

"Do you know what I mean?" she said.

"Sort of," I mumbled.

She paused. "Why am I telling you this, Paul?"

"This is a full-service station, miss," I said, standing up and saluting.

She giggled, pleased, then looked at the endlessly clicking stoplight. "Probably because you don't really have any friends."

I was silent.

"I mean, none that my friends know," she said quickly. "Friends in town, that's what I meant."

I shrugged.

She paused. "I can't tell any of my girlfriends. I can't tell my parents. And I sure as heck can't tell Stephen."

"When's he due back?"

"The Fourth of July." The stoplight clicked green. "Which gives me two weeks."

"Twelve days, actually."

She looked up at me—suddenly put her hand on my arm. "You won't tell on me, will you, Paul?"

"Never. Poke a stick in my eye."

She let out a breath. "Call Dale," she said urgently. "Right now."

Dale arrived in his Chevy at five minutes after noon. Everyone was gone for lunch except me. I had secured Peggy's station wagon in the back room, put the hood up for effect. Busy on the driveway, I saw Dale slip into the back room, and a few minutes later he came out to the pumps. There was color in his neck. He smelled of chain-saw exhaust overlaid with aftershave—he'd clearly come straight from the woods.

"Sutton," he said hoarsely. "The warehouse. Is it open?"

I nodded.

He turned away quickly.

"At one Kirk and Bud will be back," I called after him.

Traffic continued through the lunch hour, more and more tourists now. It was hotter, too, ninety degrees inside on the office thermometer. I accidentally shorted a man a dollar and he swore at me. I was barely able to keep up with the gas, let alone windshields, radiators, batteries, tires. Certainly I gave no extra service. I no longer thought much about Mr. Shell. His arrival in Hawk Bend seemed as likely as snow in July.

Quickly it was five minutes to one. Dale's Chevy still sat along the side of the station; Peggy's station wagon remained in the back with its hood up. On Main

Street I saw Kirk stroll out of the café, his right fist raised to his mouth.

"Excuse me," I called to the woman in a Ford, "I'll be right back."

I hurried to the back room, which was empty, then went through the back door to the warehouse. Its door was shut and partially blocked from the inside. "Dale?" I whispered. "Dale! Peggy!"

I could hear faint noises. I pushed on the door, and a short stack of tires moved with it. I stepped in, let my eyes adjust. And there, in the corner, impossibly contorted, on a pile of new Goodyear four-ply tires, were Dale and Peggy. Her bare, brown legs poked up like a peace sign, and there were flashes of Dale's surprisingly small white butt.

I cleared my throat and pretended to inspect a tire.

"Dale! It's Paul!" Peggy said, looking at me. She was wild-eyed and ashamed but still hung on to Dale.

"Okay, okay," he breathed—and also did not let go.

"Almost one o'clock!" I said to my tire, and carried it toward the door.

Where I could not stop myself from looking back. Dale called out suddenly, and slumped forward. Peggy lay there, panting, her eyes crossed slightly, her face shiny with sweat. I tasted salt in my mouth. Felt the hardening heaviness of my body.

At four-thirty Tim arrived, and I walked uptown for a haircut. I thought it might clear my head. I kicked a pop bottle, which clattered across the street. In the cross-walk at the stoplight someone had dumped an ashtray out his car window; a nest of yellow butts lay on the hot asphalt. I kicked at them, too. I'd had enough of the public for one day. I was looking forward to Elmo's big, deep, green barber's chair, his cool, dim shop. I hadn't been there in months.

Elmo's was a one-chair shop with a small black-and-white TV and a pile of well-thumbed *Argosy* and *Field & Stream* magazines stacked on a cribbage table. I had come here occasionally ever since I was a kid, beginning when Elmo was stout and brown-haired.

Today Elmo Pederson wore a white, eighth-inch-high flattop and white pencil mustache; he seemed old and shrunken. He stared up at the television along with three other older men, two with canes. There was some news on about antiwar protests in California. Lower, and to the right of the television, was a picture on the wall framed in red, white, and blue ribbon of Frank Pederson, Elmo's son, who had been killed in the Korean War. The colors were faded and there was dust on the ribbon.

"Sutton, is it?" Elmo nodded via the mirror. He got up and gestured to the empty chair.

"Hello, Mr. Pederson." I settled in—the chair was warm from his body—and Elmo reached back and spun me around toward the television, taped my neck with the narrow white paper, then floated the blue sheet over me all without looking away from the set. Tear-gas canisters arced and bounced and blossomed white, after which police moved forward and began to swing their sticks.

"Crack 'em good," one of the men said.

"Whack their skulls, those damn commies," said another of the old-timers.

"Why not shoot the sonsabitches!" a third said.

Then Walter Cronkite's face and his deep, serious voice came on.

"That Cronkite, he's a commie, too."

Elmo watched in silence, then reached up and turned off the sound. He spun me silently, on the great bearings of the chair, back around to the street.

"Just a trim today, Elmo," I said.

In silence, looking out at traffic on Main Street, Elmo stropped a razor.

"Draft-dodging commies," one of the older men said to no one in particular.

Elmo set aside the razor, reached to the side, to the tall jar of scissors in alcohol solution. He caught a finger loop and drew a pair out and along a towel—one swipe, two swipes—then rapped a wet comb on the counter, all without looking at my hair yet.

"Should put them in the marines," an old man said. "Send them through Parris Island."

"That'd straighten them out," another agreed.

"I didn't cry in my beer for Kennedy, believe me," one of them said.

"We don't stop the commies there, we gonna have them wading ashore in California."

"With a welcoming party of those hippies from Berkeley."

"Lucky we don't have any of those commies in this town," one said.

"You never know," another said.

Elmo began to clip my hair. He pinched sheaves of hair between his fingers and clipped away. My head kept tilting as he pulled it toward his scissors. He watched a farm pickup pass by. "What do you think, Sutton?" Elmo said.

"Just a little off all the way around," I said.

"About the war," Elmo said. "About those protesters."

I took my time. "I don't know," I finally said. "It's a tough one."

Elmo tilted my head toward his shears, kept cutting.

"Leave me a little on the sides, Elmo," I said pleasantly, glancing up in the mirror.

"I'll cut your hair, Sutton," Elmo said.

I was silent.

Elmo kept clipping. "Are you a barber?" he said.

"No."

"So I'll cut your hair, right?"

I was silent for a while.

"Have you been fishing at all?" I ventured.

"No," Elmo said. "Tourists got the lakes all fished out. I got to keep working to make a living. Up at the beauty shop they take men now. Women cutting men's hair."

"Never catch me at no beauty shop," an old-timer said.

"What about you, Sutton?" said Elmo. "Do you think women ought to be cutting men's hair?"

"I dunno," I murmured.

"Is that a yes or a no?"

"I'd have to think about it," I said.

"You think about it and I'll cut your hair, all right?"

"Sure, Elmo."

"After I got out of the army I went to barber school on University Avenue in Minneapolis," Elmo said. "I already knew how to cut hair. I did it in the army. But you had to have a license, so I got one."

The old-timers nodded.

"You need the piece of paper to hang on the wall," Elmo said, gesturing with his scissors, then homing back in. My yellow hair tumbled down the blue smock and began to build up in my lap.

"Not real short, Elmo," I said softly.

Elmo stopped cutting. He went to the wall and squinted at the framed certificate. "Well shiver me timbers, what does this say?"

The old-timers looked.

"It says Pederson here," Elmo said.

The old-timers grinned at me.

"Does it say Sutton? No, it says Pederson, Elmo Pederson. Right there. That means I'm the barber." He put the point of his scissors on the glass and tapped it sharply. Then he looked for a moment at his son, at the dusty ribbon, before returning to the chair.

"I was just telling you what I wanted," I said softly.

"What you want?" Elmo said, beginning to clip again. "What *you* want?"

I was silent.

"Whose barbershop is this?"

I shrugged. "Yours, Elmo."

"You're damn right it's mine. Now sit still—I don't want to nip your ears."

I sat stiffly in the chair. The scissors flashed at the side of my vision.

"Hard to tell the girls from the boys nowadays," one of the old-timers said.

"Ain't that the truth," the other old-timers said in unison.

Elmo brought out the electric clippers and began on my neck. I tried to swivel my head. His hand atop my skull kept me staring straight ahead.

"Elvis, he was the start of all this," one of the old men said.

I felt the clippers buzzing on my head.

"Listen, Elmo," I said. "Maybe I should—"

"Sit still. You came here for a haircut. I'm giving you a haircut. I'm the barber here, remember."

The clippers whirred above my ears. Hair kept falling like yellow leaves in September. Elmo finished, as usual, with the straight razor—a sudden splash of hot foam on my neck and a few quick swipes. I closed my eyes. Then, with a swirl of towel I was done. My head felt chilly and small. Elmo swung me around in the chair. I stared into the mirror.

"I said a trim," I said. My voice trembled with anger.

"I heard you."

"A trim. This is a flattop. At least twice I said a trim."

"Oh dear, I'm sorry if it's too short. Here, maybe this will help," Elmo said. He picked up a handful of my hair from my lap and reached to put it back on my head. I leaned away. The old-timers laughed uncertainly. Elmo kept at it, and I stood up and jerked off the blue smock.

"Take it, Sutton. It's yours. It's your hair." Elmo held out handfuls of my yellow hair. His eyes were the same color yellow—but poisoned, full of bile.

I jerked out my wallet and with shaking hands found two dollars. "Here, damnit!"

"No, no, no! This one's on the house, Sutton. It's a free haircut—like the kind they'll give you in the army, Sutton, not that you religious types will ever see a uniform."

So that was it. Always the religion. The long-necked old-timers were grinning again like buzzards. Elmo kept staring at me with his yellowed eyes.

"Go to hell, Elmo!" I said. Trembling, I threw my money on the counter and left. Outside, Main Street was a glaring, heat-baked blur. A car honked at me—braked sharply—I swore at the driver, flashed him a middle finger, and stalked on.

At the station my mother was waiting for me. As I approached she leaned forward to stare.

"Goodness, Paul! What happened to your hair?"

"Elmo." That was all I trusted myself to say.

"You got a haircut uptown?"

I nodded.

"Well, why? I'm happy to cut your hair. I always do a good job—at least I think so."

"Yes, fine, you do—but I just wanted to do something on my own, for once. By myself," I said angrily. My eyes felt hot and overly large—like they might spill over.

She stared now at my face, my eyes. I looked out my side window, caught sight of myself in the glass. My face was blotched red with anger; my hair looked like Kirk's. I touched its flat, sharp top. It felt like the face of a stiff new broom.

"I just wanted a trim, that's all."

"Elmo. He did this on purpose?"

I shrugged.

Her own jawline sharpened and she started up the engine and she pointed the truck toward Main Street.

"Where are you going?" I said.

"He can't do that to you," she said. "I hear he's had some troubles lately, but nobody should be able to do that."

"We had it out," I said. "I took care of it."

"It's not taken care of until I speak to him!" she said.

"For God's sake!" I said. My voice broke with anger and humiliation.

She braked before Elmo's shop and got out. I followed her, trotting to keep up. Just inside the door she halted. Elmo sat alone in his chair with a shaving mug in one hand and a brush in the other. He was staring at the dusty photograph of his dead son. The other old-timers were gone. He sat there in his single chair, staring. Around him, clippers, combs, towels, and lotion lay scattered on the floor. A pair of scissors was stabbed into the wall. Across the long mirror, scrawled in shaving soap, were the words "I am the barber here."

15

Tuesday afternoon, Mr. Blomenfeld's Cadillac glided to a stop at the pumps. The shiny Sedan DeVille, without Harry Blomenfeld, appeared with regularity now. Angelo and Bud had taken to having midmorning coffee together up front by the till. Angelo had an unending repertoire of jokes about "kikes," "jungle bunnies," and "spics"—"Hey, I'm a spic myself!"—not to mention cripples and Catholics—"Hey, I'm one myself!" After his visits, Bud was cheerful and chatty.

Today Harry Blomenfeld and Angelo arrived together, arguing. "So can you push the lawn mower anymore or not? Yes or no?" Mr. Blomenfeld said.

"Not that damned mower we have."

"There's nothing wrong with the mower. It's your legs that don't work right."

"I told you, I'll get at it."

"Good morning," I said cautiously.

"Paul. You're just the fellow I wanted to see," Harry Blomenfeld said. His eyes flickered to my new short hair, but he didn't mention it.

"How's that, sir?" I said. Angelo glared at me as if I were conspiring against him.

"Angelo and I have come to disagree about our lawn

and grounds—much the same way we came to disagree about changing the oil on the Cadillac."

"The car is different, damnit," Angelo interjected.

"Not in the least!" Harry said, slapping his big hand on Angelo's seat back for emphasis.

I flinched.

"Sorry, son," Mr. Blomenfeld said. "Anyway, we're wondering, Paul—"

"Speak for yourself," Angelo muttered.

"—if you might have a couple of hours once in a while to help out at the house with the lawn," Harry Blomenfeld finished.

"Gee, I dunno," I began.

"It's a lot to ask," the big man said. He had kind, brown eyes, but I noticed for the first time a sadness in them. "I know you've got your chores at home as well as your job here at the station."

"Yes, sir."

"But we need some younger legs, is what I'm saying. Angelo can drive you back and forth. Get you home."

"I suppose," I said.

"Fine. It would be nice if you could start soon," he said. He shot an annoyed glance toward Angelo. "Either that or we buy a couple of goats."

"Great—we might as well be farmers then," Angelo growled.

"There's nothing wrong with farmers," Harry said, with an apologetic glance my way. "So, Paul, when could you start?"

It was another one of those moments where I felt my life tipping in a direction I didn't even know was on the compass. I shrugged. "If it didn't take too long, I could do some mowing after work today."

At five o'clock (I'd called home, said I'd be late but had a ride) Angelo was waiting with the Cadillac. As I approached, he rolled down his window. "Your hands clean, kid?"

"Yes, sir."

"Okay, get in."

I made for the passenger's seat in front.

"No, no—in the backseat. There's a rug there for you to sit on in case you got grease on your pants."

I slid carefully into the backseat, which smelled of cigar, and closed the door. It made a sound—like a tree hitting the ground—that I felt more than heard.

"Having somebody up front makes me nervous," Angelo explained as we drove off. "I can't explain it."

I touched the leather seats, the little chrome ashtrays, then watched my hometown slide by the windows. I felt like I was president. Angelo didn't talk much—he seemed annoyed at having to fetch me in the first place—so I settled back and enjoyed the ride. Several pedestrians looked twice as the gleaming old Cadillac passed. I thought of waving but didn't.

Soon we turned slowly, and proceeded onto gravel. Angelo drove at creeping, idling speed. "Dirt roads," he muttered. "Never in a thousand years did I think I'd live on a dirt road—me, a kid from Chicago."

"I can't imagine living on a city street," I said.

"Who knows, kid, maybe you'll live in a big city."

I was silent; he looked at me in his mirror.

"That'd be strange, Angelo," I said.

"But you don't know, kid," Angelo said. "That's the good part—and the bad part—about life. You just never know . . ."

We fell silent. Angelo turned left down a narrow, pine-lined driveway. Through the trees I could see flashes of blue water. At the driveway's end was a heavy gate hung on fieldstone columns. A few of the stones had come loose, leaving empty cavities in the old concrete. Angelo got out, swung open the gate—there was a shriek of rusty iron on iron—then drove through. Used to farm gates, I hopped out.

"Hey, where you going?" Angelo said sharply.

"I thought I'd close the gate for you?"

"I'm the driver here, right?"

"Sure, Angelo," I said, and eased back into my seat, remembering similar comments from Elmo.

He closed the gate, then we drove down the curving cobblestone driveway to the main house. It was a grand old log home: dark brown, with heavy timbers notched and crisscrossed at the corners, supported by a fieldstone-and-concrete foundation. The roof was mossy in spots, and bare in others where encroaching oak branches had broomed it clean. Rain gutters grew sticks, patches of grass, and even some small oak seedlings. Beyond the house was the lawn, overgrown and shaggy, stretching down to a sagging boathouse at the shore. Big Sandy Lake was visible only in patches beyond a wild hedge and a row of trees, planted, for privacy, like the tight windbreak on my farm.

"Hello, Paul," Mr. Blomenfeld called from behind the screen door.

"Sir," I said.

"Step in. You need anything to eat before you mow?"

"Maybe something small," I ventured. I was inside by now, and looked around. It was messy with piles of *Chicago Tribune*s, and library books—at least twenty of them. Some of them were dusty—had to be way overdue. I must have been staring.

"What?" Harry Blomenfeld said.

I shrugged. "Just looking at your library books."

The place smelled like old men—meaty and woolly. Dusty taxidermy hung on the walls: a deer, two fish, an elk with a long neck and yellow teeth. It was like nothing new had touched or entered here for many years.

But the refrigerator was stocked. "Corned beef all right?"

"Ah . . . okay." I wasn't sure what that was.

I watched as Mr. Blomenfeld made me a hefty sandwich with dark bread and lettuce and pale mustard. Outside, Angelo was conspicuously loud as he rattled open shed doors and clanged gas cans and tools.

"Don't mind Angelo," Mr. Blomenfeld said. "He'll get used to you."

"I hope so, sir," I murmured. I took a bite of my sandwich. My eyes widened.

"What?" said Mr. Blomenfeld, narrowing his gaze.

I coughed slightly. "The sandwich. I've never had one that tasted like this—so good, I mean."

"You've never had corned beef?"

"Just regular beef, I guess."

"And rye bread and Dijon mustard?"

"No, sir. Pretty much just white bread that my mom makes."

He laughed largely and lit a cigar.

"Where do you get corned beef around here?" I said.

"You don't. I have it shipped in." Mr. Blomenfeld looked out the window toward the lake. "Chicago. Hog butcher, tool maker, stacker of wheat, city of the big shoulders—that's where it comes from."

"Carl Sandburg," I said.

He turned. "You know that poem?"

I nodded. "We read it in ninth-grade English."

"It's the best damn poem ever written," Mr. Blomenfeld said, slapping the counter for emphasis. "Wordsworth, Coleridge, Shelley, those English poets—they can't carry Sandburg's jockstrap."

"Yes, sir," I said.

"I read a lot these days," he said.

He glanced at his pile of library books. "Miss Verhoven, the librarian, she got me started."

"Me, too, kind of," I said.

He looked my way.

"In grade school we took trips to the library. The other kids were always scared of her, but for some reason I never was."

"I'll tell her that," Mr. Blomenfeld said, and resumed his cigar. "She'd be amused."

"I think she likes me, but she still only lets me take two books at a time."

Harry Blomenfeld puffed on his cigar, then squinted at me through the smoke. "I'll talk to her about that. There are rules, and then there are rules, you know what I mean, son?"

I didn't really, but I nodded and continued eating. We sat there in comfortable silence, me eating, him puffing on his stogie—until Angelo rattled the screen door.

"Hey—is the kid on union time or what?"

"He needed a snack, he's been working all day," Mr. Blomenfeld said.

"Well, the grass ain't getting any shorter."

Mr. Blomenfeld sighed and tipped his head toward the door. I quickly finished and headed out.

"Here it is," Angelo said, pointing to an ancient power mower. It had a windup cord on top. "It starts all right but don't cut worth a damn anymore."

I knelt and examined the mower. Underneath, the blade was blunted and nicked. "Do you have a power grinder?"

Angelo pointed toward the garage. Which, like the house, had everything it needed but was a total mess and gloomy besides. Letting my eyes adjust, I moved a bunch of junk around the grinder. I found a wrench, took off the mower blade, then returned to sharpen it. The humming emery stone breathed a stream of cool orange sparks in the shadowy garage that tickled my arms like blown sand as the blade grew an edge.

In five minutes I was mowing a clean path down toward the lake. The grass was thick as a spring hayfield, and I left small windrows of mulchy green. Mr. Blomenfeld sat on his porch, smoking his cigar and watching.

For a half hour I mowed. Beyond some heavy bushes I discovered a tennis court, overgrown like everything else. Sweating, I let the mower idle and stepped onto the court, its cracked concrete; I touched its faded lines with a grass-stained shoe. I'd never been on a tennis court before. It felt like a church without walls.

Angelo appeared. "Hey, kid, you play?"

"No," I said.

"Rich man's sport," Angelo said. "I never liked it, but the boss was a good tennis player. Used to beat everybody. Not that there were many who wanted him to lose," Angelo chuckled. "Anyway, the old man asked me if you wanted something to drink. It's hot today."

"Sure!" I said. I was sweating hard.

"Juice? Water? Beer?"

"Water is fine."

But Angelo's gaze was steady; he had not been joking. "You sure? I got some beer in the boathouse."

I paused. "A beer then," I said.

Angelo reappeared with two dripping cans of Grain

Belt. Glancing over his shoulder toward the house, he popped open the tops, then handed one to me. "The boss don't like boozing," he said, "so I keep mine down here in the lake. Perfect temperature."

I sipped the beer, my first. I wrinkled my nose at its smell—almost gagged at its taste, which was a cross between corn silage juice and burned oatmeal.

"You don't like Grain Belt?" Angelo said.

"It's fine, thank you," I managed. Grainy heat blossomed in my stomach, and gradually the beer's bad taste went away.

A half hour later the yard was mown and the hedges were clipped and I was sweaty and dirty and itching. I walked up to the house where Mr. Blomenfeld was reading on the porch. "Done," I said.

Mr. Blomenfeld put down his paper; he stood up to survey the grounds. "Looks a hundred percent better, Paul."

I wiped my streaked and dusty face.

"You want to take a dip in the lake before you go home? Looks like you could use one."

"I don't have my suit."

"Angelo, get Paul a suit and towel. And a bar of soap, too."

At lakeside I went in the boathouse and slipped into the suit. It was huge and airy around my testicles; I tried to cinch it tight as best I could, took a long sip of my beer, then made a dash for the water. It was a Minnesota lake—breathtakingly, bone-achingly cold—but it was either jump in or face the mosquitoes that had caught the heat of my sweaty body. After my cannonball I came up and splashed around. The suit was much too loose, and after a glance up toward the house, I slipped it off, hooked it to the dock. I paused for another long sip of beer, then continued paddling.

I was not a great swimmer—farm kids never were—but this evening I frog kicked, crawled, backstroked. I swam farther out, beyond the drop-off; I could feel the lake's colder darkness on my feet and calves. There, treading water, I looked back at the neatly mown lawn.

I swam farther and farther out, floating on my back—which I had never done before. Floating was more an act of faith than of skill, and I laughed at the realization, watching the puffy white clouds overhead. Then I rolled over and swam again, cutting through the chilly water like a porpoise—until I seized up like I had been harpooned.

Cramp. In one leg and then the other. I grunted as one knee came up to my belly and then the other one—fetuslike—as if all my tendons had been cut. I was, in an instant, a no-legged swimmer. And then I slipped underwater, which was enough to make me thrash, arms only, all the way to the dock. I left a wake like a speedboat with a broken prop.

I hung on to the slippery side of dock, panting, heart thudding. I rubbed and rubbed my legs and slowly they uncoiled. I looked out at the black water; at the drop-off.

"You about ready to go?" Angelo called from the yard.

"Yes!" I said. I slipped on the suit and emerged shivering and white.

"Mr. Blomenfeld will pay you up at the house."

At the door, Mr. Blomenfeld peeled off a green bill from an old-looking roll.

"Thank you, sir!" I said. Twenty dollars.

"If you treat people right, they come back," Harry Blomenfeld said.

We shook hands and then Angelo held open the rear door of the Cadillac.

I directed Angelo, via back roads, to the farm.

"Pretty out here in the country," he said, looking about, "but not for me."

"Why's that, Angelo?" He popped open another beer, and handed me one as well. What could I do?

"Too much open space makes me nervous. It's like people can see you from a long way off."

"But they can't sneak up on you either." I took a slug of my Grain Belt.

He hoisted a dark eyebrow and looked at me in the mirror.

I swallowed. "Sorry. I didn't mean anything."

Angelo shrugged. "Well, it is true, kid," he said.

At dusk farms always looked their best, especially ours. The buildings—their broad backs, their wide shoulders, their domes and cupolas—all rose up in silhouette, and the machinery, the clutter at ground level, sank in shadow.

"Nice place, kid."

"Yes." It was like I was seeing it through his eyes. I quickly finished my beer as we came up the driveway.

In the yard, I stepped out from the rear of the Cadillac. My mother appeared on the porch, wiping her hands on a dish towel.

Angelo rolled down his window. "Fine boy you have there, ma'am!" he called, and touched the brim of his chauffeur's cap. Then the Cadillac crunched gravel as it eased back down the driveway.

"Who in the world was that?" she said, staring after the car.

"The public," I said, and laughed gaily.

16

Since I had beer on my breath, I avoided my parents and headed to the barn, where I still had chores. Dave the Jailbird had taken over my garden and yard duties, but feeding the calves remained my job. Janet soon found me. "Great haircut!" she said.

"Are you kidding?" I muttered. I felt the top of my head; it bristled as tight as a garage broom.

"It'll grow back." She giggled.

"Sure. In about a year." One of the bigger calves butted away a smaller one; I rapped him sharply with my stick.

She watched for a while in silence. "I hate Is's hair. My real dad had short hair, like yours."

I looked up. "Your real dad?"

"Is is my stepdad," she said, her eyes on the calves.

"I didn't realize that."

"Most people could tell by looking."

She had a quick, sharp side to her. I shrugged. "I don't know anyone who's divorced."

She looked at me. "You're kidding."

"No," I said. I returned her stare.

She looked out the window toward the peace van.

Its rear was tilted upward. "Is and your father—mostly your father—took out the engine today."

I looked at her. She wouldn't meet my gaze.

"After I'm finished, you want to go for a ride or something?"

"On the tractor?" she said, her smile returning.

"No. The truck. I've got to practice for my driving test on Friday."

Later I drove the pickup, alone, down the lane. Beyond the gate, Janet popped out of the bushes and climbed in.

"Where to, miss?" I wore a baseball cap because my scalp still felt missing—like my brain was exposed—and now I jammed it low over my forehead.

"Central Park."

"Got it, miss."

"After that, down to Union Square and the Village."

"Roger!" I drove us, jolting, flying down the cow lane. The curving single trail threw the truck from side to side.

"Faster!" she said.

I brought the truck up to thirty, and the barbed-wire fences flew close along both sides. There was an upcoming gate, and I skidded to a stop inches from the wires. I got out, opened the gate, and we drove on.

"Once in New York this taxi driver, a foreign guy, tried to kiss me."

I looked over to her. "What did you do?"

"What could I?" She shrugged. "He tasted like curry."

I drove on. We were silent for a while.

"How far does your farm go?" she said, looking back at the buildings, which were small in the mirror.

"Still farther," I said, and pointed.

"Wow," she murmured.

I slowed alongside the woodlot, where there was an open space between two oak trees. There were tire tracks worn between the trees.

"What's this place?" she said.

"It's where I practice parallel parking."

"Can I try?"

"Have you done it before?"

"Sure," she said immediately. I didn't believe her.

"I'll go first," I said. "You watch. You can be the license examiner."

She straightened up and assumed a scowl.

I pulled carefully alongside the far tree, then backed up, trying for the perfect forty-five degree angle, when suddenly she leaned close and kissed my neck. My foot slipped on the clutch and the truck lurched backward between trees and into the brush. Limbs scraped underneath. "Jesus!" I said.

"Jesus won't help you park, Mr. Sutton." She frowned and pretended to write on a clipboard. "Sorry. You failed."

"That was unfair," I said with a stupid grin. My neck pulsed where she had kissed it.

"A good driver, Mr. Sutton, must be ready for any distraction," she said sternly. "Please try again."

I eased the pickup from between the two trees and reoriented it for another try. I kept glancing at her as I began to angle the truck backward.

"Please focus on the task at hand, Mr. Sutton," she said gravely, then suddenly slid over and kissed me again. This time she kept her lips on my neck—gave it a long, slow, sucking kiss. I swallowed, forgot to brake, and the bumper jolted against the oak tree.

"Sorry," she said, straightening up, marking her imaginary clipboard. "Another failure."

I sat at the wheel, smiling.

"One more chance, Mr. Sutton. Three times and you're out," she said in her deepest examiner's voice.

Once more I straightened the angle of the truck and readied it in reverse. I kept looking at her.

"Proceed," she said.

I began to back up.

And she began, slowly, to unbutton her blouse.

"Keep going," she said. "Nothing distracts the safe driver."

As I drove backward, she looked straight at me and continued unbuttoning her blouse. I couldn't not watch—until there was a scraping sound as the nearest oak tree jammed itself against her door. The engine died.

"Sorry, Mr. Sutton," she said in her examiner's voice. "You have failed the test." She clutched her blouse together and laughed.

I reached out for her and pulled her hard against me, harder than the oak tree lodged against the door. Then we were kissing each other all over and she was tugging at my belt. We kissed frantically, wrestling each other as if to press away any space, any air, any light between our skin.

"No, wait, let's . . ." I breathed, and only at the very last moment pushed her away. My shirt was off, my jeans tented up like a silo.

"What's the matter?" she said, drawing back suddenly.

I paused. "It's just that . . ."

"You haven't done it before?"

I was silent.

She laughed. "I have," she said. "I can teach you."

"The truck . . . we should get back," I mumbled. I could feel myself falling back toward her body. I grabbed the steering wheel and steadied myself, then started the engine.

"Okay, no problem," she said easily, and quickly buttoned her blouse.

Near the grove I stopped to let her out.

"I like driving with you," she murmured, and kissed me, hard.

I watched her slip through the trees, then I drove back into the yard, past the barn with its square-eyed windows and its tall, blank face. My head ached, and I was tired and slightly drunk and very, very lost.

17

In the morning my head ached even more. We ate breakfast in silence but for the very loud clatter of spoons. My mother was agitated, my father grave-faced. I glanced up at the clock. "I'd better get changed for work."

"You already have," my mother said, her eyes suddenly weepy.

I looked down at myself: I had slept all night in my work clothes.

At the station as I punched in, Kirk gave me a second look. "Hey, Sutton, who's the lucky girl?"

"Say what?" I snapped without turning. We got along these days, but just barely.

"Hard to give a hickey like that to yourself," Bud said.

I instantly touched my neck, then hurried into the men's room; behind me they laughed. I leaned toward the scratched mirror: high up on my neck bloomed a perfect red rose. I quickly wet a paper towel and dabbed at it—which only brightened its colors. Adjusting my collar as high as it would go, I emerged from the john. Kirk and Bud were still grinning.

"That haircut did the trick," Kirk said. "Girls don't like longhairs."

I muttered something and luckily the driveway bells sounded.

After a long day at the station, I drove the pickup into the farm shop to work on the door. The passenger's side door opened and closed, but just barely; a hinge was bent. I put on my welder's mask when I felt a presence behind: Janet and little Soybean stood in the doorway. Through my little smoked glass window they were small and far away.

"We heard pounding," she said.

I tipped up my mask. "Working on the truck," I mumbled. Light shone through Janet's long pale muslin dress.

"It's my fault, sorry," she said, tracing a bare toe in the dirt.

I shrugged. I was glad to have tools in my hands and a mask I could shrug down; I wanted to hold her and kiss her and touch her all over. "My driving test is day after tomorrow. It would be nice if both doors worked."

"If you pass and get your license, we can go driving for real!" she said.

I paused. "I'd better keep working."

"Sure."

"Don't let Soybean watch the welder's light, okay? It will hurt her eyes—like looking at the sun."

They stepped back.

I attached the grounding clamp and secured a welding rod in the other clamp; then I touched the power switch and dropped the hood. The welder buzzed, and the rod fizzed like a sparkler. A molten bead grew around the door latch, which I tapped into place as best I could with a welding hammer. Then I powered down, leaned back, and tipped up my hood.

Janet and Soybean stood there blinking. Soybean laughed and stumbled about, grabbing at imaginary butterflies of light.

"I told you not to look!" I said.

"Wow!" Janet said, waving the air in front of her eyes as if it were filled with mosquitoes. "I didn't think it would be that bright."

They watched me as I worked on, until a dusty sedan came slowly up the driveway.

"Damn," I said.

Janet looked over her shoulder. "Who's that?"

"You don't want to know."

She and Soybean slipped away as two white shirts slowly emerged from the car: Workers. They never showed up in the middle of the week. Garland Brown and Jeff Hillman stretched, looked around, then ambled to the house. I stayed in the shop and kept working on the truck. With any luck I could outlast them. However, only a few minutes later the light in the doorway changed.

"Hello, Paul," the Workers called. Framed in the doorway, they did not step in.

At the supper table, Garland Brown said grace. When the Workers came and stayed at our house, they took control of things, though not in any obvious way. One thing for sure, the blessing was even longer than my father's. Dave, weighing the effect of two more mouths at the table, leaned forward with slit eyes to count the pork chops, tally the potatoes.

Finally we ate. Bowls passed through the Workers' hands, which were soft and white. Once, Gus Sorheim had muttered that the Workers had a stupid name; I suddenly understood what he meant. A Worker was a different, inside-the-house kind of man.

During dinner Dave took the focus off me. The Workers tried to include him in the conversation, but he was too intent on eating to say much. This amused Garland and Jeff. The conversation returned to Is and his family.

"They'll be on their way soon," my mother said. "We've lent them money for their auto parts."

I looked up. Her eyes met mine; there was a grim look on her face.

"Very charitable of you," Garland said.

"Amen to that," Jeff said.

"It was more than two hundred dollars," I blurted.

"We thought it needed to be done," my father said evenly. His eyes went to me. "They've promised to pay us back when they get to San Francisco."

There was silence. "But what if they don't?" I said.

"What good is a man if he cannot be taken at his word?" my father said to me.

I looked away. There was silence in the room.

"I guess it's been a . . . different kind of summer for your folks," Garland offered. "These visitors. Dave here most days."

Dave nodded briefly to the Workers.

"And all from Paul working in town," Jeff added.

There was silence.

"More corn, Dave?" my mother said.

After dessert, I lingered at the table for what I thought was a reasonable period while the Workers helped with the dishes. They were cheerful, expert kitchen help. As clean dishes rattled and conversation between adults continued, I eased toward the door.

"Paul?" my father said sharply.

I held up my work gloves. "I should finish in the barn."

"I'll take care of it, Paul," my father said. "The Brothers want to spend some time with you."

Garland and Jeff looked my way.

"All right," I said. "I'm happy to take the night off."

No one laughed.

My parents, ever so conveniently, drove Dave back to town, which left me alone with the Workers. We sat in the living room where the window shades were mostly pulled against the low, late sun. I'd overeaten and felt heavy, sluggish, confined.

"So, Paul, how is life in general?" Garland began.

"Fine."

"And working in town—how is that?"

"Okay. No problem."

"It must have been a big change for you," Garland said.

I thought of Peggy and Dale in the warehouse, her sweat-covered face; Janet and her warm, hard peaks and valleys; the nutty, fiery taste of beer in my belly; Harry Blomenfeld and Angelo; the endless flow of customers; the click of the stoplight.

"Not so bad," I said.

There was silence.

"Well, let's turn to the Old Testament and look through a few spots, see how your reading has been going," Garland said. He opened his well-worn Bible.

I reached for mine—picked it up carefully lest dust rise from its black cover.

"No, Paul. Let's see how you do without it," Garland said, always smiling.

I put it down.

"Without the Good Book—that's how we have to live most of the time," Jeff added, "just our faith and nothing more to help us."

I nodded.

"In Leviticus, for example, what does God say about sins of ignorance?"

"They require atonement," I answered.

"What kind of atonement."

"A burnt offering," I answered.

"What kind of offering?"

"An animal?"

"It's important to read the Scriptures closely," Garland murmured.

"I think I'm better with the New Testament," I said, trying for a joke.

They were silent.

We limped through the Old Testament, and finally reached the New Testament—where I answered most of their questions quickly and with certainty.

"Well, enough of that," Garland said at length, and set aside his Bible. I let out a breath. "With a bit more work in the Old Testament, you'll be ready, Paul."

I was silent.

"A great day it will be," Jeff said expansively. "Hardly two months away."

I said nothing.

"Any more questions about the Bible, then—or about the faith we share?"

"Yes, actually."

Jeff Hillman straightened up eagerly.

"The Old Testament seems pretty strong on punishment of sins," I said, "while the New Testament is more about forgiveness. On giving people another chance."

"Yes, you're right," Garland said. "Good."

"So which one are we supposed to live by?" It was a question I hadn't thought of until this moment.

"That depends, Paul."

"On what?"

"On you, Paul."

I was silent. "You mean I get to choose?"

"In a way. Kind of," Garland said.

"Well, then I'd scrap the whole Old Testament," I said suddenly.

Their eyes widened.

I swallowed. "Well, not entirely. You know what I mean."

"I'm not sure that I do, Paul!" Garland said. His smile was gone for good. "The Old Testament gives us many rules to live by—including the Ten Commandments."

"That's another thing," I continued.

"Good, Paul," Garland said; his teeth glinted white in the dusky room.

"Thou shalt not kill—but what about in war?"

"That would certainly be excluded," Jeff answered.

"What about in self-defense? Say someone like that guy in Nebraska, Charles Starkweather, tried to get into our house and I shot him?"

"Doubtless that would be justified in the eyes of God."

"Okay. But what if you were an old man who had killed people when you were younger, but felt bad about it, changed your life, and were a good person after that? Would you still go to hell?"

"That sin of murder is nearly impossible to erase," Garland said.

"No chance," echoed Jeff.

I thought of Mr. Blomenfeld. His kindly, sad eyes. "Okay," I said.

Garland peered closer at me; I manufactured a smile.

"Do you have any other questions, Paul?" Garland said.

"No," I said with certainty.

Garland Brown glanced at his younger companion, then back to me. "I'll be honest, Paul: Your parents are worried about you."

"And we are, too," Jeff added.

I remained silent.

"It's not easy growing up these days. The sin and squalor, the temptations of this world."

I held my poker face.

"Do you have any questions for us about that?" Garland said.

"About what?"

"About becoming"—Garland Brown coughed—"a man?"

"You mean, like girls and sex?" I said.

Garland Brown tugged at his tie and glanced through the window. "Yes," he said, "that."

"No, no questions."

"Well then," Garland said with relief, glancing at Jeff. "Let us have a short prayer to finish."

There was silence. They waited.

"Will you lead us, Paul?" Garland said finally.

I mumbled a short lame prayer about thankfulness for all things, then said, "Amen."

And was released.

18

On Friday, my sixteenth birthday, at eight a.m., I took my behind-the-wheel test. The examiner was Mr. Grussing, a middle-aged man with a crew cut who taught accounting at the high school. He wore a short-sleeved white shirt and flip-up sunglasses. Assuming I would pass the test, my mother and father waited off to the side in our other vehicle.

"Name?" Mr. Grussing asked.

"Paul Sutton."

He signed something on his clipboard, then had trouble with the passenger's side door.

"Recent accident?" he said, settling into the seat.

"Oh no, sir. Many years ago," I said.

He pursed his lips, then shut the door.

"You have to slam it," I said.

Fifteen minutes later, I pulled back to the same curb. My mother gave a discreet and encouraging wave, but Mr. Grussing, sunglasses still down, stared at his clipboard. Then he flipped up his glasses. "Mr. Sutton. Where did you learn how to drive?"

"Driver's training."

"Here in America? Or in some foreign country?"

"Here, sir. And then I drive around on the farm quite a lot."

"Well, it shows."

I took in a breath. "Did I pass, sir?"

"Let's put it this way, Sutton. The lowest possible passing score is seventy points. In school terms, that would be a D–. Your score, Mr. Sutton?"

"Yes, sir?"

"Seventy."

I fought back a victory yell.

"Technically you passed, Mr. Sutton, but you have more bad habits than I've ever seen in a young driver."

"Sorry, sir."

"You know who you drive like, Mr. Sutton?"

"No, sir."

"You drive like an adult. We teach driving with two hands; you drove mostly with one hand, and seemed to have your mind on other things—like adults."

"I'll be a careful driver, sir, I assure you. I won't let you down."

He narrowed his eyes at me, then signed off.

And I was free! An emancipated sixteen-year-old!

"Congratulations, Paul," my father said, and shook my hand. After that my mother clamped me in a hug.

"I have to go to work," I said, extricating myself, but there was time for one loop down Main Street. I motored along slowly, window down, lifting one finger from the steering wheel in greeting to local pickups, nodding and smiling to tourists, who looked at me oddly.

After a brief drive about town, I turned back to the station, which, in the space of an hour, had grown smaller. I was comfortable there now; I knew its workings as well as I did the farm. There was nothing about my job that I couldn't handle. With Bud on duty in my absence, I drove fast up to the pumps—made the bells *dinga-ding, dinga-ding* like a pinball machine. Bud came out the door, annoyed, then drew up at the sight of me.

"Did you get it, kid? Did you pass?"

I gave him the thumbs-up.

Bud saluted. "Look out, world."

That night, after helping my father with some welding on the corn cultivator, I showered and put on a clean T-shirt and jeans. "I was thinking of driving into town and getting a root beer," I said casually to my parents. My mother was tidying the kitchen, my father was reading the newspaper. There was a brief silence. They looked at each other.

"Well, I guess you do have your license," my mother replied.

I nodded.

"All right. Don't be gone long," my father said.

"Watch for deer on the highway," my mother said. She followed me out onto the porch. "And bring back some root beer for us."

Then she turned away and purposefully did not look again—as if this were just another warm summer night on the farm.

I drove down the winding driveway, looking in my mirror back to the house. As my parents stood silhouetted in the screen door, my father put his hand on my mother's shoulder. Then I passed beyond the windbreak and out of their sight—where Janet was waiting.

"I passed," I said, and threw open the door.

She laughed and scooted all the way across the seat, where she leaned against me. Her hair smelled clean and fresh.

"Where to, miss?"

"Anywhere, fast!"

At the highway, I revved the engine, spun from gravel onto blacktop. Janet laughed with delight and tuned the radio to WLS, where we sang along to Martha and the Vandellas' "Dancing in the Street."

At sundown, Hawk Bend put on its night face. Dusty pickups and motor homes retreated to farms and lakes; hot rods and muscle cars rumbled into town, along with teenagers cruising in their parents' Pontiacs and Fords. Paused at the stoplight was Kevin Hemstead, a kid in my grade, driving a 1962 Chevy four-door on which he had put shiny, baby-moon hubcaps. When the light turned green he managed a chipmunk chirp of his rear tires.

"Pathetic," I said to Janet, trying to hide my envy. I thought of putting my arm around her, but didn't.

"Let's go down Main Street," she said.

I joined the slow crawl of cars in the center of Hawk Bend. Knots of teenagers stood in front of the pool hall, whistling greetings to passing cars. Girls darted out, laughing, and leaned into a driver's side window. Traffic paused without complaint, then moved forward again. Competing music sang from radios and eight-tracks: Elvis, Buddy Holly, Patsy Cline, the Beatles, Bob Dylan, the Animals.

After two loops down Main Street, we headed south of town to the A&W drive-in. It was past sundown now, the western sky bloody red from heat and dust, and below its colored lights the drive-in swarmed with cars and kids. I parked under the end of the awning, lucky to find a spot, and touched the intercom button.

"The carhops are actually on roller skates," Janet said.

"Yeah, so?"

"I thought that was, like, something they made up about the Midwest."

"Real carhops, real skates," I said. A tinny, girl's voice came over the little speaker; I ordered two root beer floats.

"For here or to go?" There was laughter inside, glass clinking, and the sharp hiss of burgers hitting the grill.

"Here," I said. I would get my parents' root beer just before leaving town. That way it would still be cold when I got home.

Janet and I sat listening to music and watching drive-in life. Close up, two large moths flopped and fluttered in the overhead yellow lights, and smaller insects swarmed the buzzing orange A&W neon. Carhops came and went, their skates clacking over seams in the concrete. The parade of cars thickened. Kirk's blue Chevy looped by; his wife, Lynette, sat very close to him with one arm draped around his neck. Kirk's face was fixed with a look of part defiance, part shame. As he sized up cars and carhops, his eyes caught sight of Janet and me: he lifted his chin in the faintest nod of recognition as he drove past.

"I wish you had a fast car," Janet said.

We sipped our floats and listened to music until a throaty rumble of engine drew our eyes. It was Dale Bender's 1955 Chevy. At idle speed the big 409-cubic-inch engine ran rough and phlegmy—like an old male lion trying to clear his pipes. Still in gray primer paint, the two-door Chevy had tinted windows all around; on the driver's side, a white T-shirt sleeve stretched tightly over a massive biceps, and a thick, darkly tanned forearm held up the roof.

"Wow, who's that?" Janet said.

"Dale Bender. Fastest car in town."

"It doesn't look fast."

"Dale's car is deceptive," I said. "That's what I like about it. The engine and running gear are all built up and reinforced." I started to tell her more, but as the car pulled in I saw close beside Dale the flash of a white sleeveless blouse, a bell of blond hair with its perfect flip.

"Jesus," I murmured.

"Don't get all hot and bothered, it's just a car," Janet said.

Dale parked at the far end, in the shadows, then

rolled up his window most of the way (the other window, even in this heat, was fully closed). Janet turned to the radio, looked for a new song. I sipped my float and kept my eyes on the 1955 Chevy.

"So what are we going to do tonight?" Janet asked.

"I dunno," I said distractedly. Eventually a carhop skated toward Dale's car carrying two tall root beer floats—to go. Dale briefly rolled down his window to receive the drinks. Inside, wearing sunglasses and leaning on Dale's big shoulder, was Peggy Leikvold.

"What is it?" Janet said.

"Nothing."

"It's like you keep seeing things," Janet said, looking around with annoyance.

Dale's window went up again and the big engine coughed alive. The Chevy eased from the A&W and onto the highway—Dale blipped his engine once to remind us losers of our pathetic vehicles—and then, without smoked tires or undue attention, purred away south of town, beyond the streetlights and into the falling purple sky.

Janet and I sat there a while longer. I finished my float. "Come on," I said. "Let's go."

"Where?" Janet asked, rattling her straw with a last suck.

"I don't know," I said.

"Back down Main Street," she said. "I love cruising."

I slowly dragged Main, idling through its heat and

music and shadowy throngs of teenagers and the red glow of their cigarettes. We made two loops.

"Now where?" I asked. I glanced at the time; I still had to get the root beer for my folks.

"Anywhere," Janet said. She pressed close against me, put her breath on my neck. I turned on a side street and drove slowly, block by block. It was dark now, and she melted against me; I put my arm around her, kept the truck moving. "Is there, like, a lovers' lane?" Janet murmured.

"Kind of," I said.

"So?" she breathed. She touched my neck with her lips.

I turned into the boat landing at Hawk Lake just north of town. To the sides it was dark and forested; faint moonlight trickled through tall pines. Here and there, parked for a lake view, were the black slumped shapes of a half dozen cars tucked in shadows alongside a clump of trees, all several car lengths from one another. I coasted to a stop at the far side, punched off the lights. "Look," I said to Janet, pointing to the half-moon both above and on the water of Hawk Lake.

She didn't; I could feel her smiling at me.

"This is where they shoot off fireworks on the Fourth of July," I said. I was suddenly tongue-tied.

We made out until our lips were bruised and our bodies ached all over—at least mine did, and in one spot in particular. Finally, at the last moment, I pulled away, caught my breath.

"What's the matter?"

I checked my watch. "We should go," I said.

Coming into Hawk Bend, I saw Kirk's car still circling Main Street. I cut over a couple blocks, avoiding the stoplight and the Shell station, then I drove east, beyond the city limits and toward home. Janet clung to me all the way, kept her head on my shoulder. At the windbreak I coasted to a stop. She looked up at the farmstead, the faint orange flicker of Is's campfire. "It feels like I live here," she murmured.

"You do, sort of."

"Not for much longer," she said, and tipped her head against me.

I kissed her again, hard, and then she slipped out.

As I eased the truck past the yellow yard lamp, my mother came onto the porch. Beyond her, at the kitchen table, Dave sat in my spot eating a large bowl of ice cream.

"You were gone nearly two hours," she said. My father appeared behind her in silhouette.

"Sorry," I said to them. "Guess I lost track of time."

As I came into the porch light she looked me up and down.

"It felt good just driving around," I explained.

"By yourself?"

"Yes," I said. Lying came easier nowadays.

She was silent for a moment. "And our root beer?"

19

On Monday morning, Tim, the night man, walked into the station.

"You're a little early," Kirk said. There was a lull in traffic; Kirk, Bud, and I stood in the front office by the till.

Tim grinned oddly; his face was whiter than normal. "Last night my old lady had a miscarriage."

"Jesus," Bud murmured.

"I'm sorry," I said. I tried to think of more and better words, but failed.

Kirk clucked his tongue once, then looked out to the street.

Bud offered, "I didn't even know she was knocked up."

"Us neither," Tim said, looking at us with a lopsided grin. "She was in the bathroom, and then she let out a scream."

We were all silent.

He turned to get himself a soda, fumbled in his pockets for change.

"Your money's no good here," Bud said. He stepped forward and opened the pop cooler with his key.

Tim snapped off the cap from a bottle of RC cola.

"She said she was feeling funny, then she went into the can and pretty soon I heard her screaming," he said. "It was about this big." He held up his free hand and made a fist; it trembled slightly.

Outside the driveway bells rang.

"I got it," Kirk said quickly, and disappeared.

Tim leaned back on the counter and stared out at the intersection. "What the heck—easy come, easy go, right?"

We were silent.

"Is she okay?" I asked.

"In the hospital," Tim said. He looked away, down the highway. "Which is why I stopped in. I should go hang around there tonight with her," he said apologetically. "At the hospital."

Bud glanced at me.

"We'll cover your shift," I said. "Don't worry about it."

"What, me worry?" Tim said. He reached behind both ears and pushed them out, elephantlike.

Bud and I stared.

"Alfred E. Neuman. *Mad Magazine*, get it?"

Bud and I managed a short laugh. "That's good," Bud said.

"Very good," I agreed.

"I'll be back tomorrow night just like always," Tim said. "I'll be here."

"Sure," Bud said.

We watched him walk away and get in his battered

little Chevy. He didn't start the engine. He lit a cigarette and sat there smoking and staring through the windshield at the cars that passed, at the stoplight that clicked and clicked.

And so I took my first evening shift: five p.m. until midnight. Between shifts, I walked uptown for supper. At Paula's Café I ordered a roast beef plate with mashed potatoes and gravy and green beans and apple pie. I didn't drink coffee, but Paula automatically set a cup in front of me. I sipped it. With cream and sugar it was not half bad.

In the corner above the till was a TV, with the sound turned off. B-52s flew in formation and dropped their bombs, black teardrops that shrank away beneath the planes, went out of sight for several seconds, then blossomed into white flowers in the jungle far below. Closer in, helicopters flew low and sprayed pale streams of fire. The picture cut to an interview with Nguyen Cao Ky, the new premier of South Vietnam. He was a smiling, tidy man who wore a French-style beret; Paula paused by the television and turned up the volume slightly. Ky's English was hard to follow, and the restaurant was noisy, but I caught the gist of it. The war was going well. Very well, in fact. It would soon be over—only a few more months.

"Like hell," Paula murmured.

"Order!" the cook called.

Paula moved on, then brought a full plate my way. "Here you go, son," she said. She paused to look at my haircut. "You going in the army or something?"

"No," I said.

"Good," she said.

I dug into my food. I was hungry—but I'd hardly gotten started when someone slid onto the stool next to mine. "What say, Sutton?"

It was Stephen Knutson—Peggy Leikvold's real boyfriend (maybe "real" wasn't the right word anymore)—Stephen Knutson, who was supposed to be out of town. My recent afternoon on the hot seat with the Workers had been good practice for my poker face. I nodded his way. "How's it going?" I said. I kept chewing.

He squinted at me. "I'm not sure. Maybe you can tell me."

"How so?" I cut a square off my breaded roast beef, popped it in my mouth. Knutson was bigger than me, and had a Corvette, but guys like him didn't impress me anymore.

"I understand Peggy comes into the station."

"Her dad has a charge account."

"And Dale Bender? He comes in, too?"

I shrugged. "Once in a while, I guess."

"They ever come at the same time?"

I took a long sip of my coffee. I hated lying. "Maybe. Yeah."

"They talk, or what?"

"I guess," I said evasively.

"I knew it," he muttered, then cursed and looked through the window.

I kept eating.

He swiveled back to me. "Word has it Peggy has been riding around with him in that Chevy."

"Dale Bender, you mean?" It was like he had difficulty saying the name, but I didn't.

He nodded.

I shrugged. "Hey, I just work there," I said, and took a huge mouthful in order not to talk.

Knutson rearranged the salt and pepper shakers so they were side by side. "So what, you a sophomore now, Sutton?"

"Yes." When I turned back to him, he was smiling weirdly. A flat, fake smile.

"That's a fun grade. You'll like it."

I shrugged.

He picked up a sugar packet, flipped it hand to hand several times. "Got your license?"

"Yes."

"Got a car yet?"

"Working on it," I mumbled through my food.

"Ever drive a Corvette?"

I looked at him. "Can't say as I have."

"They're something else," he said. "Quickest cars around."

"Maybe," I said.

He stopped moving on his stool. "Hey, nobody in this town can beat me—for sure not that heap Bender drives."

I was silent.

"Anyway, want to drive it some time?" Knutson said.

I turned. His eyes were overly bright and jerky.

"Me?" I said. I coughed once—a shred of roast beef down the wrong pipe.

"Sure. You got a license. Why not?"

I shrugged. "Okay. When?"

"Right now if you want."

I checked my watch. "I might have a few minutes," I said.

"I'll get it," Knutson said to Paula, and took my dinner check.

When I settled into the driver's seat of the Stingray, it felt like I was sitting on the ground. I looked out my side window; cars towered above me. Inside, the cockpit wrapped around me like a rib cage. My hand fell naturally onto the stick shift, its hard round knob.

"Standard four-speed with a lift-up, lock-out for reverse," Knutson explained.

I nodded.

"Go ahead," he said. I fired the engine.

"Wow," I murmured, my poker face long gone.

"A full 365 horses," Stephen said. "Let's get out of town and you can run through the gears."

Carefully I drove north past the station. Kirk turned his head as the Corvette grumbled by; Knutson did not look—purposefully it seemed. I concentrated on moving smoothly through the gears.

"Nice," Knutson said. "You're a natural."

In each gear the horsepower felt like a big hand on my lower back shoving me forward.

"Take a left," Knutson said. "We'll head up to the strip."

I knew where that was. Everybody did. Three miles north and west, just beyond the lake, was the flattest, straightest strip of asphalt around, perfect for drag racing, but with an additional feature. The land on both sides of the highway was mainly bog and low brush; thus there were no homes or farms—no busybodies to call the sheriff—and the sedge had saved lives in the occasional rollover. There were only a few trees of substance, and those were well past the finish line. Both start and finish points were marked by a slash of white paint across the highway. The distance between the two marks was exactly 1,320 feet—a quarter mile. Every spring the local highway department painted over the white stripes; by the Fourth of July, fresh lines reappeared.

"Full stop," Stephen said. "Let's see how you are off the mark."

In first gear I brought up the rpm's; eased the clutch up halfway while holding the brake with my toe. The Corvette hunched its back and leaned forward.

"Now!" he said.

I torched the tires for fifty feet, then smoked them again in second gear, and again briefly in third. In seconds we were going ninety miles per hour, the swamp brush a blurry tunnel of green. I backed off well before the finish line.

"Hey, we were just getting going!" Knutson shouted.

I could not keep a grin off my face.

"Like I said, great car, eh?"

"No kidding," I said, tapping the brakes as we slowed, then coasted.

"You want a Corvette, you should have one," Knutson said.

I looked at him. He was not joking.

I checked my wristwatch. "Listen, I gotta get back to work."

"Sure," he said. "Pull over. I'll drive."

We traded places and headed back to town. "Anyway," he said at length, "about Peggy. I want you to keep an eye on her."

I stared ahead through the glass.

Knutson looked at me. "There are a lot of creeps around. Creeps like Dale Bender."

"It's busy at work," I said. "It's not like I have a lot of time to keep track of everybody."

"But you see everybody who drives by," Knutson said. "You know everything that goes on in this town."

"Not everything," I said.

"Plus she likes you—"

I turned to him.

"Thinks you're a nice kid, is what I mean."

"Right," I said drily.

"So if she says anything, goes anywhere—and Dale Bender's involved—I want to know," he said. "That's all."

I was silent.

"I'll make it worth your while," Knutson added.

"Like how?"

He had that odd smile on his face. "Later this summer I'll be going to orientation down at the U," he said. "The Corvette will just be sitting in the garage. You could take it for a few days."

I looked at the cockpit, the stick shift. "Are you serious?"

"Hey, why not? You already passed your test run." He laughed too loudly.

I said nothing.

"Good then, it's a deal," Knutson said, and slapped my knee. "Hey, here we are, kiddo."

I got out at the station drive and watched the Corvette chirp rubber back onto the highway. Bud came out. "Wasn't that Stephen Knutson?"

I nodded.

"What'd he want?"

"Take one guess," I said.

Traffic that evening was endless. On duty alone, I did the best I could, running gas and checking oil and scrubbing bug spatter from windshields. At midsummer, the remains of insects were thicker and more colorful: heavy-bodied beetle parts with red-and-yellow blood, summer flies with long pale bodies, furry wings of giant moths, grasshopper heads as hard and shiny as marbles— so many insects that radiator grilles caked and cooling systems ran hot. I realized I could not help everyone; I could not get to them all. At one point a customer left before I could wait on him.

For the first time in days I thought of Mr. Shell. He was featured in the latest company newsletter along with a kid in Michigan who won a thousand dollars by fulfilling the seven-point code for Mr. Shell. There was a photo of the kid shaking hands with Mr. Shell who, "in order to hide his identity," had his face blacked out. Mr. Shell was not a big man, not a small man; he wore a short-sleeved shirt, no tie, and had no distinguishing moles or tattoos on his arms. "Mr. Shell is always on the move," the article read. "He may arrive anywhere, on any day, at any hour. Are you prepared to give full service—and more?"

The driveway bells dinged; it was only a car full of tourist girls.

Later that night, Stephen Knutson's Corvette appeared. He turned sharply into the station. The hardtop was off, and Peggy Leikvold rode with him. Knowing she was on display, she sat low in the seat, and stared straight ahead. She wouldn't look at me.

"Fill it, ethyl," Knutson said. He had on strong-smelling cologne, and paid no attention to me. I took my time on the windshield, but Peggy wouldn't look up at me either.

"Charge it," Knutson said, and left with a squeak of the tires. I wrote up his charge slip, then returned to another customer. I was crouched behind a battered Ford when I heard the rumble of Dale Bender's Chevy. Its wide-set yellow eyes grew from the north, then swung into the station.

"You seen her?" Dale asked. "I was supposed to meet her tonight."

I stared. Dale was cleaned up and his hair gleamed and tumbled in a dark waterfall. He wore the same after-shave as Knutson. Around me the air was suddenly humid and close.

"You just missed her," I said.

His dark eyes brightened with pleasure. "What was she driving?"

"Riding," I said. "With Knutson."

Dale's face went blank. Then his eyes shrank to the hard shine of beetle shells. "Did she say anything?"

I shook my head.

"Which way did they go?"

"I was busy. I didn't get a good look."

He cursed, then shifted into low gear and rumbled up to Main Street.

A full hour later I had three gas hoses running when Knutson's Corvette came back into town. Directly behind him, a yard off his bumper, was Dale's Chevy.

"Hey, kid, you gonna check my oil?" a customer called from his station wagon.

"In a minute," I said.

"Anytime would be fine."

I ignored him. Knutson and Dale slowed for the

stoplight, which, as it had to, turned red. Dale swung into the opposing lane, which, as it had to be, was empty. Dale looked past Knutson to Peggy, who would not turn. Her cheeks were shiny; she was crying. Dale revved his engine—a deep-throated bark of horsepower. Stephen Knutson's Adam's apple bobbed, then he brought up the Corvette's rpm's. For one long moment everything in Hawk Bend paused.

When the light clicked green, the intersection heaved. Blue smoke billowed from wheel wells and both drivers wrestled their steering wheels to stay straight. Knutson left early, but Dale made up ground through first gear. I hurried toward the street to watch them go. The Corvette and the older Chevy howled north side by side, Dale in the wrong lane. Oncoming traffic veered to the curb as both cars smoked their tires in second gear and slewed dangerously close. The Corvette had the better transmission, the quicker shift; Dale had more horsepower. In third gear he slowly drew ahead—a bumper's width, a half-car length a full-car and then two car lengths. He swung in front of the Corvette. Knutson hit his brakes. He darted left, down a side street, and Dale's big Chevy slung itself straight on for several more blocks before it could brake and turn. By then Stephen Knutson and Peggy were gone.

"Damn kids!" a customer squawked. "They'll kill somebody." He was balding and sat in a dusty station wagon; the backseat had been chewed on by kids or dogs. I topped off his tank.

"Ten dollars even."

He waited. "Aren't you forgetting something?"

I stared at him.

"My oil?"

"Sorry." I popped his hood, pulled the dipstick.

"And get my windshield, too," he called. "I thought this was a full-service station.

20

The Fourth of July weekend loomed; fireworks were set for Saturday night. Tim's wife continued to bleed; I continued to work overtime. The sun did not set until nearly ten o'clock, and in the heat no one slept well—except for Dave, who sawed logs down the hall from my room and got up several times a night to use the bathroom. His jail term over, he was staying with us—until he "got his bearings," as my mother put it. I didn't really mind; I was hardly ever home.

At the station, tourist traffic rose toward a crescendo. Mr. Davies hired a part-time kid, Eugene Siskin, whom I trained for the night shift. He could not handle two cars at once and only made my job harder. I taught him the seven-point code, and warned him of the possibility of Mr. Shell's arrival. But my heart was not in it.

As the week wore on, the double shifts wore me down. Driving home from work on Wednesday night, I braked the truck hard and skidded sideways to avoid flapping crows and a white picket fence—but found only black asphalt patches on the highway and the orderly white stripes of the center line.

On a hot Thursday night, toward closing, Dale Bender's Chevy passed through the intersection. Its dark tinted windows were fully closed but I was certain I saw a smudge of blond hair behind the smoked glass. Friday night Dale himself came alone to the station. "How's it going, Paul?"

"It's gotta go," I said.

He smiled briefly, and lit a Lucky Strike. I squinted at him in the streetlight. His eyes were bloodshot and tired, as if he hadn't been sleeping.

"I been thinking, Paul."

"About what?"

"About Peggy. After I leave."

"When do you go?"

"Two weeks. Leave from Fargo on the bus."

"Jesus, Dale," I said. I felt weepy for some weird reason.

"Hey, get a grip, Paul. You ain't the one drafted."

"Sorry," I said. "Tired, I guess."

"Here," he said, shaking a single Lucky Strike half out of the pack, and holding it out to me, "you need a cigarette."

"No, thanks."

He laughed. "What—you think you're gonna live forever?"

I paused, then took it.

Later that night I slipped out of the house to meet Janet. We found each other along the cool, curving concrete side of the silo. Neither of us said anything—we crashed together and kissed until we couldn't breathe.

Afterward, we slipped around the barn and down the lane in the moonlight. She pulled away and ran laughing ahead of me. I caught her—a clumsy tackle—and we fell into the hay field, onto a sweet-smelling windrow of alfalfa, and lay there kissing until the mosquitoes found us. They tickled and pricked our skin. We swatted them as best we could, but with our arms entwined, our hands busy elsewhere, the mosquitoes escaped, drifting from Janet to me, me to Janet. When we did kill them, they left little black smears on our pale skin. The blood could have been hers, could have been mine.

"We have to keep moving!" I said, and we ran, outpacing the mosquitoes for at least a couple of minutes.

"Fireworks Saturday night," I said.

"I love fireworks," she said, taking my hand.

"We'll go together."

We walked on in the moonlight, in silence.

Then she stopped me and said, "Is and your father have the engine almost back together."

"Maybe it won't run," I blurted.

We stared at each other, then Janet began to cry. We leaned up against a tree and kissed, and let the mosquitoes take us.

On Saturday afternoon the old, the handicapped, the lonely, and parents with carloads of whining kids began to arrive in town to position themselves for the fireworks—which were not until ten o'clock at night. It was always a contest to see who secured the best parking spot at the Hawk Lake landing. Fireworks were shot from a barge moored just offshore.

"Pathetic," Kirk muttered as traffic in town thickened. "It's like they've never seen fireworks in their sorry lives." Eugene Siskin had quit, and Kirk was pressed into service at the gas pumps. Luckily, Tim was back on duty, so I punched out at six, and sped home against heavy incoming traffic to get Janet.

And her family.

"Sorry—they all want to come," Janet whispered, as Rising Moon rounded up the children. Janet's face and neck were spotted with bright red mosquito bites (I had them like chicken pox).

"Can we ride in the back of Paul's truck? Can we, can we?" the children shouted.

"Why not?" Is said. The kids looked healthier now—tanned and fuller in their faces. They all scrambled aboard.

"We'll find you there," my mother called from across the yard. Dave already waited by the car. It was like he was one of our family now—the older, prodigal brother come home. If so, what did that make me?

The drive from the city limits sign to the landing took a full twenty minutes. "An actual traffic jam," Is called. He stood up in the rear to see better, and his tie-dyed T-shirt and bushel of black hair drew stares. But not for long; people were too busy having fun. Music played from car radios and tape players, and ahead the smell of hot dogs and burgers wafted from the parking lot where the local Jaycees had set up their brightly painted food trailer. Nearby was a competing trailer belonging to the Elks Club. I found a good parking spot on a side hill and we all clambered out. Below, at the landing, kids splashed and chased dogs in the water.

"Can we? Can we?" called Safflower and, without waiting for an answer, grabbed the toddler and ran toward the shore.

"I better go keep an eye on them," Rising Moon said, and followed.

"They'll be fine," Is said as he continued to stare at all the farmers and tourists.

"What a crowd," Janet murmured.

Is surveyed the scene. "Sad."

"Why sad?" I said.

"It's sad how deeply people have bought into the whole patriotic load of crap."

I shrugged. "Patriotism is not all bad."

"Wait till you get drafted and sent to Vietnam—then you'll change your tune."

I was silent.

"Farm boys like you from small towns, poor black and Hispanic kids—that's who the government wants for their war machine. You're perfect, and you know why?"

"No. Tell me," I said sarcastically.

"Because you haven't been politicized. You have no awareness of global issues. You haven't started to think."

"For once just shut up!" Janet said.

Is blinked and drew back.

"Come on, Paul," she said, and tugged me away. We found a spot on a grassy bank by a tree, which put us above the sea of people on their blankets and in their lawn chairs. She leaned against me. We didn't talk as we watched the people. The sun settled toward the far lakeshore and twilight rose dusky, smoky; the air drew grays and blues from the lake.

"Soon," I said, slipping my arm around her.

"I can't wait."

"For what?" I teased.

"Why, the fireworks, of course; what did *you* mean?" Through my arm tight around her I could feel her smile.

And then the opening shot: *Ka-boom!*

The crowd cheered in one voice. Fireworks arced and hung—a sudden bleed of color quickly healed by the purpling air. "Oooooh! Ahhhh!" went the crowd at each shot. I lost track of time. Holding on to Janet always felt better than anything I'd ever done in my life. Eventually a red, white, and blue flag of fire—with heavier concussions—brought everyone cheering to their feet.

"That's it," I said.

"Are you sure?"

"Yes. Grand finale."

"How do you know?" she said. "Let's wait."

We did, but there were no more fireworks.

In the parking lot we met up with my parents. Janet

and I held hands defiantly, brazenly. "I want to stay in town for a while," I said to my parents.

"Me, too," said Janet.

The two sets of parents stared at us. Safflower sing-songed, "Janet-loves-Paul, Janet-loves-Paul."

"Just shut up!" Janet said.

Is and Rising Moon laughed; my parents didn't.

"Hey—it's the Fourth of July in middle America," Is said. "Let the kids have some fun."

"But not too much fun," my mother said. She stepped forward and touched my face—as if to protect me, inoculate me from this midsummer night—then turned away.

As the crowd flowed past, Janet and I waited in my truck and listened to the radio. Janet laughingly pulled me down onto the seat, out of sight of passersby, and we murmured and touched each other until the landing was quiet. Janet popped up to look. "Everyone's gone," she whispered; she sank back down, took my hand, and held it to her breast. I left it there for a burning moment, then pulled away. "Not here," I whispered. "If we're going to do it, we should do it right."

"You mean it?"

I paused a moment. "Yes."

"When?"

I turned up my face to hers; I could see stars through the windshield above me. "Tomorrow night."

"Where?"

"I'm thinking, I'm thinking."

"Somewhere" (kiss) "without" (kiss) "mosquitoes," she said. And we made out until the stars moved, until the Big Dipper rose in the northwest sky.

Much, much later, as we came home I shut off the truck's engine well ahead of the house and we coasted into the yard. Even the dog didn't bark. Is was still up, silhouetted by the embers of the fire ring.

I walked her home, so to speak—to the van and the fire ring. Is looked up. His eyes were slitty in the orange glow, and he was smoking a hand-rolled cigarette, which he cupped in his palm as we approached.

"Well well, if it isn't the lovebirds."

"I'm going to bed," Janet said. She blew me a kiss, mouthed "Tomorrow night," and disappeared into the van. I smiled and turned to go.

"Hey, Paul, what's the rush?" Is said.

"It's kinda late."

"Too hot to sleep."

I was silent.

"Let me ask you a question."

"All right," I said.

He looked up at me. "Do you believe all that Bible crap your parents lay on you?"

I paused. "Bible crap?"

"You know what I mean." Is motioned for me to sit down. I glanced over my shoulder to the darkened house.

"The Bible runs their lives big-time," he said, "but what about you?"

I shrugged. "I dunno."

"A reasonable answer," Is said. He took another puff and stared into the fire. At length he said, "But the question remains, doesn't it?"

"What question?"

"The main one, the big one, the heaviest one of all: Is the Bible true?"

I was silent. I crouched by the fire, poked it briefly with a small stick.

"Your parents think it is. Certainly, so do those Workers who are after you. But what do you think?"

I shrugged. "I'm not sure. Maybe some parts are, some aren't."

He took a puff of his joint, handed it to me. I knew what it was, and if I had not already had a cigarette from Dale, offered in the same, easy motion, I would not have taken it. But I did. I took a short puff—coughed once—and handed it back. It tasted way sweeter and better than a Lucky Strike.

"I used to believe," Is said. "The *whole* Bible, I mean—which was a little strange for a Jew. But then as I got older and saw how the world really works, how crappy and unfair things are, I came to think that none of it was true—that God gave up on us."

"Which means He was there at some point," I said.

Is smiled. "Very good. You got me there." He

handed me the joint; I took a longer draw. I did not cough this time. "So you do believe," he said.

I slowly exhaled. "I guess. Sort of. I mean, somebody had to get the world started. Nothing can come from nowhere."

"Okay, I'll go for that," Is allowed. "But what do we do about Jesus? God is pretty simple to explain; it's Jesus who creates the problem for us."

The fire shifted, glowed, snapped briefly; we thought about that. Gradually there were two campfires, then three. I touched the ground to steady myself. "Listen, I should go," I said.

"Sure," Is said absently, and didn't look up.

I headed across the dark yard, which suddenly rose in small hills, sank in deep valleys. My stomach churned, and I hung on to the prickly caragana hedge—and threw up. Afterward, I crossed to the milk house, where I splashed water on my face. I slumped there for a while on the cool concrete until I felt better, then passed through the swinging door into the barn. I had chores. I was certain that Dave had not fed the calves—that they were starving, possibly dead. I fumbled with a single lightbulb chain overhead. In the sudden light, black-and-white calves stood up sleepily and blinked at me. Milk bottles lay here and there, but I unlatched the gate and went into their pen to make sure; they didn't rush me, which was a good sign. Dave had even put down fresh straw—way too much, but better than too little. I held a handful to my nose: it smelled like baked oats, like August. The calves milled about now, and the pen tilted—threatened to spill all of us, so I latched the gate. I sat down among them. Sat on the clean straw and leaned against the battered wood and squinted my eyes at the fly-spotted little sun that swung slowly overhead. I heaved up and caught its chain, turned off the light. The calves soon quieted, and I closed my eyes—just for a second. I listened to sounds of the night barn: the purr of pigeons in the hayloft, the skitter of mice overhead, the whisper of stars as they swam through the dark ocean of the sky, the pale froth of the Milky Way.

21

Sour, stale breath in my face. A raspy tongue licking my arms. "Paul, Paul—wake up!" I opened my eyes —saw straw, muddy black hooves, fresh calf dung—and Dave's long potato face close to mine.

"Whaaaa?" I said. Dave hoisted me into a sitting position. Butch the labrador kept licking.

Dave leaned closer, his rank breath in my face again. "Your father's here. You don't want to let him see you like this."

But it was too late. I struggled to my feet, covered with splotches of fresh calf dung bearded with straw, my shirt stained with vomit from last night. Something— probably more manure—caked one ear. My father leaned on the side of the pen, watching.

"Well, Paul," he said. "You've hit bottom."

"I—I was just checking on the calves last night," I began, but my throat was dry and my tongue thick and I couldn't find any more words.

"No need to explain," he said. "After you didn't come in last night, I had a long talk with Is, then found you here."

"You found me here?"

"Yes. I thought it'd do you good to sleep it off."

"Jesus," I said.

"Dave, get him into the milk house and help him clean up—it's time for Meeting," my father said.

I squinted out the window; the sun was bright in the smudged panes; I could see cars in the yard. It was Sunday, the Fourth of July.

"He'll need some fresh clothes, won't he?" Dave asked.

"No. Get the worst of it off him, and bring him—just like that."

Dave looked at me uncertainly, then back to my father, who turned away. "Come on, Paul, let's go," Dave said. He held my arm as I walked along the alleyway, past the stanchions on either side.

"I can walk," I said. We moved as if in slow motion.

Dave pointed down the gutter on our right. "That's the bottom," he whispered hoarsely, with a glance over his shoulder. "Your old man thinks you're there, but you're not even close."

In the milk house I got cleaned up as best I could, and then we crossed the yard to the house. Mrs. Halgrimson's car, closest to the front door, had her front tires well onto the lawn. Ray Swenson, smoking in his car, nodded gravely at me as I passed, as if we were old friends.

Inside the living room twenty faces, all the usual ones—the VandenEides, the Grundlags, the Sorheims—turned to stare. There was a sucking in of breath from several adults, a nervous rippling giggle from the VandenEide sisters, and soft sobbing from my mother. Dave helped me get seated near the door. I winked at the nearest VandenEide girl, who wrinkled her nose as she smelled me. She nudged her closest sister, who, like dominos falling, pushed them all down one chair. After much rustling and clumping (Mrs. Halgrimson slid her chair closer to my mother, and held her hand), the first hymn began.

Dave's rank breath kept me awake as he sang along, but then I didn't remember much until chairs clattered. The VandenEide girls, each holding her nose, gave me a wide berth on their way out. "You're in big trouble now, Paul!" the oldest one, Mary, whispered as she passed.

Which was not untrue. When the living room was empty, my mother clamped on my ear and hoisted me toward the stairs. "Get up there, take a bath, then go to bed. We'll talk about this later—when you're able."

"There's still a little dung in your right ear," Dave said helpfully.

I took my bath, and scrubbed myself all over, then sank into the clean, fresh white sheets. I dreamed not of Peggy and me, but for the first time of Janet. I saw us in the dim, sweet-smelling hayloft, our clothes spread around us like offerings, our bodies like open pages in a dark-covered book, soft paper rippling in a warm breeze.

As I slept, a couple of times I thought I heard loud voices in the yard, the sound of cars, engines, thudding doors. However, I did not know what was real and what was my dream, so I slept on. When I awoke, much later, the light had changed in my window. I stumbled across the room and looked out onto our yard.

It was empty. The yellow van, the tent, Janet—all were gone. The only proof they had been there was the dark eye of the fire ring, and the last wisps of its smoke rising into the twilight air where they thinned and disappeared.

22

Dave the Jailbird was right: I had not yet hit bottom. After Janet was gone, soon Dale left for basic training, and then Peggy went off to the university (with Stephen Knutson, who never followed through on his Corvette offer). I stayed on at the station. I smoked cigarettes, and I drank beer with Tim the night man, for whom would I pinch-hit on occasion.

Sometimes when I was alone at night, moving quickly from car to car with no time to put money in the till, my breast pocket bulged with a wad of cash. When time permitted, I rang up the gallons, deposited the money. Once, after closing, I found ten dollars still in my shirt pocket. I was driving home, and remembered that it was for some Shell No-Pest Strips, which were not under inventory. I promised myself I would return the money in the morning but I didn't. After all, I worked hard—way harder than Kirk or Bud. I deserved a bonus.

Gradually I began to keep a few dollars every day. Occasionally I "borrowed" a new tape for the eight-track player I'd bought for the truck. I slit the cellophane wrapper with a razor blade, extracted the tape, and played it. When I tired of it, I carefully replaced the tape in its original package. I took rum-soaked Crookette cigars without second thought. My crime was made easier because Kirk was stealing, too. I had started to notice his attention to the tire warehouse and its inventory; I was never permitted to count tires. He was a good tire salesman—especially when Mr. Davies was gone. Kirk talked tourists out of their perfectly good tires and into new ones by using a shiny penny. Tires were all about tread depth: less than five thirty-seconds of an inch was in "the danger zone," which Kirk illustrated by pinching a penny up to the tip of Lincoln's head, then holding it close to the befuddled customer's eyes. "I mean, this amount of tread will *probably* get you back to Minneapolis," Kirk would say. "It's up to you." He gave substantial discounts for cash, and in this way acquired excellent used tires, which he sold on the side. Once, when a foursome of good used Firestones came in, Kirk said, "Hey, Paul, wouldn't a pair of those fit your truck?"

"Probably," I said.

"Go ahead, put them on—my treat."

I did, and Mr. Davies was never the wiser. I told my father I'd gotten them for a steal. The knowledge that Kirk and I were complicit was a kind of balm between us, and diluted the bad blood of earlier in the summer.

If I worked a night shift, I drove around for a while, usually by myself, but sometimes with girls whom I saw hanging around the pool hall, girls with strong-smelling hair spray and cigarette breath. A couple of times they wanted to go to the Hawk Lake landing and park, but I pretended indifference, pretended I had better things to do. In truth, none of them measured up to Janet—or to Peggy, for that matter.

I also stopped Bible study with the Workers, and I sat at Meeting in the back row with my arms folded and did not sing the hymns. Then, early one Sunday morning in August, the phone rang. It was Bud from the station.

"Paul—I hate to call you on Sunday, but Kirk finally got his in a vise with somebody's husband. He's on the lam for a day or so until the guy calms down. Tim can't cover for him and I can't either. Could you come in?"

"Okay," I said. I put on my Shell uniform in silence, and walked past my parents and out the door.

Sunday morning was not a difficult shift; nobody needed tires or an oil change or their muffler fixed. Mainly it was families stopping on their way home from church to top off the gas tank and buy a newspaper. As I attended to them, I inspected their clean clothes, their church dresses, their suits and ties, their Sunday hats. Tidy families. Families who belonged to things. Fathers who were in the Jaycees, or Rotary, or Elks. Mothers who were elementary-school teachers and volunteers at the old-age home.

In the middle of this, Mr. Davies himself drove up. "Paul! I'm very sorry," he said through his open window. He parked his car and came over, grabbing a fresh chamois cloth on the way. "I promised you you'd never have to work on Sunday, so I want you to head home. I'll take over."

"Really, it's no problem," I said, but he would hear none of it.

"A promise is a promise," he said. "And please apologize to your mother for me."

Suddenly I was free on a Sunday morning, in town.

Across the street the second Lutheran service was in progress, the sound of its choir falling sweetly from its open windows. I walked to my truck, paused, then suddenly passed it by. I went across the street and up the sharp granite steps of the church. At least I had on a bow tie. The usher, an old man, handed me a program in silence and pointed to the side entrance, back pews. I slunk inside, sat down.

The church was as big as our hayloft. It had heavy-duty curving rafters that held up the roof, polished wooden pews with seat cushions, an ornate carved altar, a preacher with a microphone, and at least a couple hundred people in the audience. When the choir stopped, the preacher said something—which everybody answered in one voice. This startled me. I looked in the program, but couldn't find where they were. This went on, the preacher speaking, the people answering, without pause or silence between. It was loud and moved fast. Then the preacher launched into his sermon. I glanced around. Most people appeared to be listening, but with the glazed look I'd seen on my father's face at Meeting when he was especially tired. To pass the time, I paged through the hymnal. Some of the songs I vaguely recognized, but most were different, some in Norwegian, and the music to them looked dense and complicated.

Thankfully the preacher finished, and there was rustling as everyone straightened up. People in the first rows stood up and walked forward to take communion—which was my cue to slip out. The usher had nodded off on the bench outside, so I made a clean escape back into sunlight and fragrant summer air.

I had a sudden strong desire to get home, fast, and I sped most of the way. I thought I might make the last part of Meeting, but met Mrs. Halgrimson's and the others' cars as they departed.

Inside, Dave was folding up the chairs with sharp clacking sounds.

"Sorry," I said to my parents.

They turned to me.

"For everything," I added.

My mother's face softened. "You missed your breakfast. You must be hungry, Paul."

"I am," I said, but for what I didn't know.

23

I reached an uneasy truce with my parents, but by then the summer was almost over. Toward the end of August, Hawk Bend began to dry up: the grass browned along the boulevards, the leaves on the elm trees shrank and dulled, and tourists—exhausted by tents, cabins, bugs, and bad mattresses—packed it in. They arrived at the station in droves, their sunburned children slumped in the back reading comic books or stretched out asleep, and made sure I checked their oil, radiator, battery, and spare tire.

And suddenly, it was time for church camp, or "Convention," as we called it. I had thought of not going, of volunteering to stay home and take care of the farm. But Dave was there now, and generally trustworthy with the cows, so there was no real reason for me to stay home.

The drive to southern Minnesota was long, as it had been throughout my whole growing up, but never this long. I chafed. I shifted. In the backseat I tried to sleep but couldn't. I was used to music in the pickup; to the ding of the station's driveway bells; to the rattle of pneumatic tools; to the laugh and giggle of summer girls. Now there was silence in the car except for the tire sounds and my parents' intermittent and predictable conversation.

"It's so nice to have Dave around so we can get away for Convention," my mother said for at least the third time.

"A blessing," my father agreed.

"And for the whole Convention, too," she added.

Mother glanced back at me. I lay slumped over in the backseat, half asleep. Thanks a lot, Dave. Convention for five full days. It seemed impossible. With every small town we passed my real life—Peggy, Dale, Janet, Harry Blomenfeld, Angelo, Bud, Kirk, the summer girls, the unending stream of the public—slipped farther away, receded like smoke, like a dream. As my father drove on, I had the weird sense of growing younger, of reverting to childhood, of actually shrinking in size. I closed my eyes to dam up, to secure all that I had gained this summer.

I opened them again, groggily, reluctantly, when my father tugged my arm. "We're almost there, Paul."

I sat up in the backseat. On the gravel road we followed the dust of another car, and there were more cars and pickups ahead of it, all turning up a long, flat, farm driveway that led to the grounds, which at first sight to a stranger must have looked like a county fair: Sunlight glinted off long rows of vehicles, all neatly arranged by young male attendants wearing white shirts and holding colored signs. Beyond the field parking lot were several long white two-story wooden buildings that surely must be 4-H barns and craft buildings. At the center was a larger, square building, most likely the arena for rodeos and livestock competitions. And just beside it, the tall green canvas sides of the circus tent where the band certainly played and elephants trumpeted and trapeze artists swung. But what to make of the women all wearing long skirts? And the men carrying Bibles? Look, even the children have Bibles!

Every year a few people actually mistook the convention grounds for the county fair or a circus, which was a source of great amusement to the Faithful. In truth, the long white buildings were dormitories, two for men, two for women. The bigger white building was the main meeting hall. The giant green tent was the food tent, where meals were cooked and served. The Bibles were Bibles.

"Up ahead—park on the left," one of the parking boys called. He was a serious-faced young man who wore a short-sleeved white shirt damp with sweat, and his arms were pink with sunburn. "God bless," he said.

"Praise be," my father answered, and drove on.

We parked. The engine died.

"Well, Paul, we're here," my mother said. There was a note of triumph in her voice.

"I can see that," I said. I rubbed my eyes as if I were still sleepy, but I was not. I felt myself go on some kind of watch—some kind of alert. I needed to be on guard, though against what I wasn't sure.

We carried our suitcases and bedding, plus a gunnysack of new potatoes. As we moved through the crowd, my parents nodded and smiled to this one and that. The VandenEide girls passed. Their thick hair, braided and coiled into wings on each side of their heads, and their tittering, jerky movements reminded me of a flock of chickens ranging across a farmyard. When they saw me they giggled. The older one, Mary, wore her skirt a few inches higher than her sisters. "I told you he'd be here," she said to the others, and gave me a triumphant smile.

I ignored them.

"Paul, where are your manners?" my mother said.

I scanned the crowd, hoping there was no one else I knew.

At the side door to the cook tent we waited in line with our food offering. Ahead of us other people moved forward with peach crates full of shiny glass jars of dill pickles, apricots, blue plums; others held gunnysacks of sweet corn, boxes of orange carrots, tubs of yellow rutabagas. From the doorway, arms of male Workers reached to take produce and pass it hand to hand back into the giant pantry. One set of arms, with some actual tan to them, belonged to Jeff Hillman.

"Greetings, Suttons!" he called out animatedly. He waved. "Welcome, Paul!"

I nodded once. Workers were never so lively and cheerful as at Convention, which was annoying. But perhaps this was their time, their reward for life on the road. For at least a few days they were home—maybe the only true home they had—and in the company of others like themselves.

"We're having a young folks' special meeting tonight," Jeff called to me. "Seven o'clock, Paul? See you there?"

My parents looked encouragingly at me.

"Okay, okay," I muttered.

After making our food offering, we went to find space in the dormitories. My mother surprised me by pausing to give my father a quick kiss—right there among the crowd—before she moved off to join the other women. My father watched her go. Some women called her name and smiled broadly in greeting. My father turned.

"Well, Paul, we're on our own."

I shrugged.

"Let's go find us a spot," my father said. Everything—his every word—annoyed me.

The older dormitory where we usually stayed was full, so we were directed to a newer, Quonset-type building. Inside, as with the old dorm, were wooden sleeping compartments not unlike stalls in a horse barn, except here the second story was open; ladders ran upward to a second level of bunks where younger boys laughed and hung over the sides to peep at their fathers or drop bits of straw on friends passing below.

"You want to be up?" my father said.

I shrugged. "Okay."

We continued down the gauntlet of giggling boys. Every few yards was a wash station—a basin, small mirror, and a plug-in for electric razors (the toilets were in a separate building just outside)—until we found a space at the far end. Each compartment had a straw tick; we had our own bedding.

"This should do," my father said cheerfully. He, too, seem livelier, more energetic. "Climb up and check it out."

I did.

"Suitable?" my father asked.

"Sure."

"Catch!" he said, and tossed up my little suitcase and then my bedding.

As I arranged things, my father spoke with other men; they asked about the crops in our area, about the harvest. Most all were farmers. The upper level was open, without walls, and spread out in a sea of straw ticks where younger boys tumbled and dove like seagulls. One gang of ten-year-olds bounced my way; they were sweaty and laughing. "Hey, you want to play?"

"Beat it," I said.

They stared, then laughed at me and somersaulted on.

At the special meeting for youth, I took a seat at the rear. There were about forty or so kids, most of them at least two or three years younger than me. Great. I felt like an eleventh grader in sixth grade. Jeff Hillman and a younger woman Worker, who introduced herself as Gretchen Radamacher, were cheerful and outgoing. Jeff's cheeks were flushed with more than sunlight. How could Workers go through life without touching, kissing, holding another person? I didn't believe it was humanly possible—not for a minute—and I watched the pair with suspicious eyes and a hard heart.

"I hate this," a voice muttered. I turned. Mary VandenEide sat two seats away. With her hair in wings like her sisters' but with brighter blue eyes, she glared at the chattering Workers and the usual teacher's-pet types up front. "It's stupid."

"What do you mean? It's good for you," I said.

"Shut up, Paul. If anybody needs this, it's you."

"And what about you?" I replied.

Mary bit her lower lip to hold back a grin.

"Now then, we're going to do skits from the Bible, from scenes you all know," Gretchen Radamacher called out. She was not unpretty, with pale blond hair held up in back with heavy black combs. "We have parts for everyone. We just need some volunteers to get us started."

Hands waved. Mary Contrary crossed her arms over her chest and slumped down in her chair. "What are you smiling at?" she said to me.

"Nothing," I said.

"But first we're going to sing a few hymns," Jeff said, sitting at the piano.

There were audible groans.

Later, as the fourth song droned on, Mary Contrary tugged my sleeve; I might have been dozing slightly. "Look what I've got," she mouthed.

I blinked and turned. She glanced about, then cracked open her Bible case. In it was half of a cigarette.

My eyes widened. "You're going to get in trouble," I mouthed back.

She set her jaw, cupped the cigarette stub between two fingers, and pretended to sit there smoking.

"Big trouble!" I added.

"Not any more than you," she said defiantly. I ignored her, and soon enough she put away the butt.

We sat there and watched the Goody Two-shoes act out scenes from Exodus. Mary Contrary and I were forced to participate in the crowd scenes, and chose to be oppressed people on the march. We circled the room with the others.

"Great acting!" Gretchen Radamacher said as Mary Contrary and I came by. "Everything about you two says 'slaves.' "

Mary and I snickered. When I looked up, Jeff Hillman was watching us; he was not smiling.

After the meeting I met up with my parents. The sunlight was low and tawny by now, and the old-timers were already heading to the dormitories.

"How'd it go?" my father said.

I shrugged.

My mother glanced around. "I've seen a few boys you know," she said. "You're welcome to go play for a while."

" 'Play'?" I said instantly.

"Sorry, Paul!" she said quickly. "You know what I mean. Socialize."

But the damage had been done, and I succeeded in annoying my parents by staying close by them until the ten o'clock whistle blew, which meant we had a half hour to get into bed.

So to speak.

I had no complaint against straw ticks. They were fine to sleep on so long as the straw was generally new (old straw ticks turned flat and dusty) and were plumped beforehand. At Convention it was the night noises that took getting used to. Tonight I lay in the heat and darkness with my eyes open. Here and there fathers "shussed" young boys—murmured sharply at them— which brought muffled sobs. Old men snored suddenly and deeply, like huffing, chugging engines switched on. Soon the youngest boys, too tired to cry, exhausted by racing about the grounds just before dark, joined their higher-pitched throat noises to the old men's rasp and drone. Completing the choir were the fathers—I could hear mine below—whose snoring came last. The combined chorus rose up the curving, cylindrical walls of the Quonset building and gathered in the highest point of the roof, directly above my tick, then radiated downward as if from the dome of an opera hall.

A great, sweltering corrugated-metal opera hall. Large fans at either end—one for intake, one for exhaust—hummed ineffectively. Sweat came onto my forehead and the small of my back. I tossed and turned well past midnight.

In the morning came the slap of the old men's straight razors on leather strops, and soon the sharper *tack-tack* of the same razors rapping on tin basins. I groaned and tried to sleep again, but after the old men came the buzz and snarl of electric razors—my father's in particular—and I tossed and turned until he called my name.

I waited in line at the wash station to splash cold water on my face and give my teeth a cursory brush, then headed outside (the morning was already warm) to the bathroom, a long, low building with a concrete floor and a trough—a gutter—along both walls, themselves fronted by corrugated aluminum. I found a narrow space between the other men, closed my eyes, and did my duty. The smell of morning urine was hot and strong, like ammonia.

Afterward I looked for my father. Beyond the bathroom building was a path that ran down to the river. Often men walked down there to talk, or to read their Bibles along the banks. As a kid I played there with other boys, but, luckily, today I spotted him nearby.

"Hungry?" he asked.

We crowded in line at the food tent to wait for the first breakfast whistle. Men talked and laughed. Boys like myself and younger stood slumped and squint-eyed. At the short blast of the steam whistle we flowed inside.

Beneath the tall green dome of the tent we secured two spots and waited as the long tables filled up. There was seating for close to three hundred. On the tables, plates and bowls and cups were facedown, as always. A small bell rang and the hum and buzz of voices went silent. Far up front a single Worker sang grace—after which, like the sudden cheering following "The Star-Spangled Banner," there was a roar of clattering dishware. I had always liked this moment, and today, with my exhausted hard heart, was no exception. Down the grass aisles Workers and their helpers rolled carts heavy with vats of oatmeal, racks of bacon, tubs of yellow scrambled eggs, sheaves of toast, urns of steaming coffee. Jelly and syrups—all home canned—salt and pepper, all the rest of it was on the table. Bent over my plate I ate as if I had not eaten for weeks.

Afterward, as the clattering slowly rose from those who were finished, I wanted only to take my full belly back to my straw tick and sleep all day. But no such luck. In a half hour, morning Meeting began.

That day and the next and the next were endless, dreamlike. I did not sleep well at night, ate too much too rapidly at meal times, and felt groggy through the sermons, the hymns. Once I actually slumped against my mother, who let me doze on her shoulder. I awoke a full hour later with her arm around me, and felt rested for the first time in days.

On Saturday the sermons were not the worst in the world, particularly the one by Garland Brown. A few of the Workers were "closers," that is, could be counted on to pick up the crowd even after several days of the

Gospel. The best of them allowed a small joke here and there, and laughter rippled from the podium even to the back walls of the great hall.

Where, I noticed, Mrs. VandenEide sat grimly with Mary Contrary (the rest of their family was up front).

On the way out after a dull afternoon meeting, I whispered to Mary, "So, you in trouble or what?"

"No. I just won't sit up front."

"Why?" I teased.

"I hate people looking at me."

"What makes you think everybody's looking at you?" I liked to provoke her.

"Because they know I'm supposed to profess this year. Just like you," she added.

Our eyes met. Hers were angry, and blazed with blue light.

By Saturday evening I'd begun to feel strange. Different. The angry, annoyed feeling was mostly gone; I began to pay attention to the sermons. I felt more awake, and began to follow along in my Bible with some of the readings—which, if given a chance, had some fairly useful things to say. My life had quieted, and in the space and silence I began to see my town life from a great distance—as if my job at the station was something I'd read. During certain hymns, ones I'd always liked as a child, I felt odd and weepy.

After the Saturday evening meeting, Gretchen Radamacher singled me out. "I've enjoyed getting to know you a bit at the youth meetings," she explained.

"And we like to meet as many of the young folks as possible. Would you like to take a walk?"

"Ah, okay," I said.

So we joined the slow promenade of strollers on the long driveway. The loop was from the convention grounds to the county road—but not onto it—and then back. She was easy to talk to, and I was soon telling her things.

She listened. "Life gets complicated," she offered.

"But not for you," I blurted.

"Sometimes, I think, especially for me," she said. "This life isn't always easy."

We kept walking.

"But we do the best we can, we pray hard, and usually God gives us the answer," she finished.

I felt her looking more closely at me. I glanced away. And saw, approaching us, Jeff Hillman walking with Mary Contrary. He was doing all the talking. Mary clutched her Bible to her chest and did not notice me.

Sunday dawned humid and close. I had not been able to sleep well—awoke even before the old men. By getting up early, at least I did not have to pee in the presence of fifty old men. My splashing echoed eerily in the long, rank concrete corridor. When I emerged, the grounds were still empty. The grass between the buildings and beside the cook tent was ruined, bare in spots, though not muddy because the dry weather continued. It was too early to eat, so I took a walk around the grounds.

The main meeting hall was open, but cavernous and vacant. I walked on, thinking about life, my sinful life, one of secrets and deceit. I turned down the path to the river and soon enough stared at its shallow flow. It was a no-account river—nothing like the clear streams up north—slightly muddy and only waist deep, but here, this afternoon, I could have all the bad things in my life washed away. Cleansed. Gone. I began to shake and freeze. Goose bumps came onto my arms. I felt lifted out of my body and whirled around; I felt dizzy and backed away from the shore so as not to fall in. I sat down, took a breath, gathered my wits, and headed back to the main grounds, and then to the parking lot. For a while I could not find our car, could not remember at all where we parked. A panic came over me. I began to trot, then jog up and down the rows.

Then I drew up and stared. In one of the cars, two young people were wrapped in each other's arms, kissing frantically. Even the car swayed. Sunburned arms, a white shirt on a white blouse—it was the parking-lot boy and Mary VandenEide, whose long hair, even as I watched, came loose from its combs.

And then came the final service of Convention. It was a time when all the songs, all the sermons of the preceding days gathered like waters in a narrowing channel, and moved with increasing weight and force. I felt both sweaty and chilled. The Meeting passed in a blur of song and sermon.

And suddenly it was Garland Brown, introducing the last hymn. "We close, as always," he began, "with the opportunity for those among us who have not accepted Jesus into their lives to do so now . . . to stand and be counted."

The Workers began the hymn, and soon came the chorus:

> *Softly, tenderly, Jesus is calling*
> *Calling for you and for me . . .*

Here and there chairs scraped. One by one, across the great hall, people my age stood up. Tears streamed down their faces as they made their way to the front. Hands patted them as they passed; parents wept for joy. I felt a tide of grace, of exultation, a kind of light actually lift me from my chair: I stood. My mother sucked in a breath.

Once standing, I felt the same tide, like an undertow, draw me toward the aisle, the straight and narrow pathway to the front, to the smiling preachers, and, afterward, baptism in the river. Then I saw Mary Contrary. Head down, plodding resolutely toward the front, she passed me obliviously, her face streaming bitter, defeated tears. And I sat down.

24

On Labor Day, my last day at the station before I quit for the school year, I put in two shifts. There was a final surge of traffic, mainly retired people who owned cabins and milked the last juice from summer before heading home. These older drivers were the worst kind of customers. Check the tires. Check the windshield wipers. Check the brake fluid. Check the spare. Check the valve stem in the spare.

Which I did without complaint. After Convention, some kind of horizon had shrunken. Drawn itself closer to the present, to the moment at hand. I began to think more about small matters: the right socket for the right nut; oiled threads that turned one way only; the brightly colored odor of gasoline. I put my faith in the wide steel arms of the old hydraulic hoist; an oil can's pouring spout and warm, olive flow; my pocket feeler gauge and its polished, wafer-thin fingers with which I gapped ignition points and set valve clearances. I took pleasure in the perfect pitch of an engine in tune, in the absoluteness of tools.

This carried over into how I approached people as well. Regularly I drove out to Mr. Blomenfeld's estate and mowed the lawn. Once, as I arrived, I saw Angelo and Bud duck into the boathouse, and another time I found Miss Verhoven, the librarian, having dinner with Harry Blomenfeld. I accepted this. I made no judgments, offered no gossip. Everyone around me—the customers, Kirk, even my parents—I took at face value. The world was made up of people and things, things and people. That was it. I took comfort, felt a kind of oneness with everyone and everything that went on around me, because I understood that I was on my own: how my life unfolded was up to me.

Kirk, Tim, and I labored all that day until near closing, when traffic died as if the roads around town had been rolled up and stored away. "I'll close up," I said to them. "Why don't you guys take off." Since Convention I had quietly been punching out an hour or two early, then staying on to work. It was a way to pay back Mr. Davies for the stuff I'd stolen.

"You sure?" Kirk said. Tim was already heading to his car. His wife was home, healthy now, and, as Tim put it, "back in the saddle."

"Sure. I'll drop off my key tomorrow."

"Hey, keep the key. We might need you on occasion this fall. And you're coming back next summer, right?"

"That's a long way off," I said.

"Well, it's been real," Kirk said. We shook hands, and he turned to his shiny Chevrolet and motored off uptown (not home).

I sat on the station steps before the empty intersection and smoked a last small cigar. The stoplight clicked, and clicked, and clicked. The churches on three sides stood somber and still. I finished my cigar, then checked my watch—fifteen minutes left. I locked up the back room, gave the johns a quick mopping, then emptied the windshield-washing buckets by the pumps and rinsed the tattered chamois cloths. I went inside to power down the lights—was reaching for them—when the bells rang.

I swore briefly, tiredly, and went out. A dusty station wagon sat at the far pumps. Some family getting a late start back to Minneapolis was my guess, though I couldn't see anyone but the driver.

"Evening. Fill with ethyl?"

"Five dollars regular," the man answered.

Not "Fill it up" but "Five dollars." For the full-service attendant, this was the most annoying request; it meant that I had to stand there and watch the spinning numbers—there was no time to move around, wash the windshield, check the oil. "Sure," I said.

I finished the gas, then went alongside the open window. "Anything else?"

"I guess that's up to you, kid." In the shadows, I couldn't get a good look at him, but he was clearly your average pain-in-the-butt customer.

"Let me get that windshield," I said.

"Thanks. Bugs are bad tonight."

I went for a fresh sponge, wet it, trudged back to his station wagon. He was my last customer; it felt important to go out on a high note, to do it right. When I finished the glass I said, "Oil all right?"

"Check it, would you?" He stepped out to watch me—the kind of guy who didn't trust anyone—but I was okay with that. Each to his own. I pulled his stick, wiped it clean, reinserted it, withdrew it for his inspection. "Good," he said.

Before closing the hood, from habit I made sure the radiator cap was tight, the battery cables secure, the windshield washer reservoir full, the fan belt tight.

"Five dollars," I said. He fished out a twenty (of course), so I headed to the office. Passing behind his car, I paused: the left brake light was out. Had it been earlier in the day I would have gone back and alerted him. Changing a taillight bulb was a five-minute job, maximum. But he was in no real danger, I was tired, and the summer was over.

I came back out with his change. "Thanks," I said.

He seemed to pause, then from the shadows said, "Looks like it's closing time—is the men's room still open?"

"Right over there." I pointed the way. Inside the office I swept the floor and watched the drive, hoping the lonely station wagon wouldn't attract another car. The man stayed in the bathroom a long time—what do they do in there?—but finally he came out and started the engine. His lone brake light blinked once, then he caught a green light and drove away west.

Inside, I shut down the main bank of lights over the pumps—*kachick, kachick, kachick*—then went around to lock the doors. In the men's room, stuck between the door and the frame, was a folded piece of paper. I pulled it free, opened it.

At the top was the official Shell logo and a checklist of the seven-point code. All were checked except "Extra Service." My heart started to pound in the back of my skull.

At the bottom, handwritten, were these words:

> *Good job, son. I was pleased, especially since it was closing time. But I know you saw my brake light, and that was the extra service I was looking for. Sorry, but the rules are the rules. However, I'll be giving you and your station (very clean bathroom, by the way) a positive report in general.*
>
> *Sincerely,*
> *"Mr. Shell"*

I drove straight home, though I didn't speed. My truck radio was picking up Little Rock as clear as a bell, but then it faded, replaced by WLS from Chicago. The Beatles' song "Help!" came on, and I listened to it as if for the first time. At home, I parked the truck, then sat on the porch and watched the stars. The days were shorter now, the sky dark, and the constellations were never brighter. Suddenly I laughed—at the great, cosmic hugeness of things—at how small this porch was, this house, this farm, this township, this county, this state, this whole planet.

My mother came onto the porch in her nightgown.
"Paul, you're home!"

"Yes," I said. I kept looking at the Milky Way, and the galaxies unending.

She sat down beside me. "How'd it go tonight?"

"Fine."

"So you're done for the summer."

"Yes."

She was silent.

"By the way, thanks," I said.

"For what?"

"For sending me out there."

She stared past our driveway to the dark road beyond, then bent her head. "I didn't think 'out there' would be quite so far."

I put my arm around her; always it had been the other way around, but tonight I hugged her close. "I'll be okay, you know."

She looked at me, then we sat there watching the stars.

"There's Orion." I pointed. "See his shoulder and, below, his belt buckle?"

"Kind of . . ." she said. "It's something I should do, learn my stars."

"We'll get a book, figure them out together—every one," I said.

"Okay, I'll try," she said, then shivered. "I'm going in. Do you want anything, some ice cream?"

"I'm fine," I said, and really I was. I stayed on the porch after she left, looking up into the sky. I lay back to take it all in. The night was a giant domed tent, shot with salt or white sand, and through those tiniest of holes shone a huge light, one that people never got to see. But no doubt about it, it was up there, behind everything, burning on and on.